THE
LIAR
IN THE
LIBRARY

SIMON BRETT

BLACKTHORN

First published in Great Britain, the USA and Canada in 2019
by Black Thorn, an imprint of Canongate Books Ltd,
14 High Street, Edinburgh EH1 1TE

Distributed in the USA by Publishers Group West and in Canada by Publishers
Group Canada

First published in 2017 by Severn House Publishers Ltd,
Eardley House, 4 Uxbridge Street, London W8 7SY

blackthornbooks.com

1

British Library Cataloguing-in-Publication Data
A catalogue record for this book is available on request from the British Library

ISBN 978 1 78689 486 1

Typeset by Palimpsest Book Production Ltd, Falkirk, Stirlingshire, Scotland

Printed and bound in Great Britain by Clays Ltd, Elcograf S.p.A.

THE
LIAR
IN THE
LIBRARY

Simon Brett worked as a producer in radio and television before taking up writing full-time. He was awarded an OBE in the 2016 New Year's Honours for services to Literature and also was elected a Fellow of the Royal Society of Literature. In 2014 he won the CWA's prestigious Diamond Dagger for an outstanding body of work.

simonbrett.com

To Alicia,
with love
from Ong Noi

ONE

A nd I think it's very important for a writer to have a secure emotional base at home. In the solitude behind one's desk one travels a roller-coaster of ideas and impressions, so it's good when one returns from the wilder shores of the imagination, to be able to settle back into a reality in which one feels grounded. And I am fortunate to have found that emotional grounding with my wife – not my first wife; many of us make mistakes when we are young and foolish (SMALL CHUCKLE) – but the right wife. In my case, Persephone.'

The speaker's words prompted an only-just-audible sigh of satisfaction in Fethering Library. His audience, mostly female and mature, felt comforted by avowals of marital love. Particularly when they came from a writer as eminent as that evening's guest, Burton St Clair. They knew, from their reading of the *Daily Mail*, how often fame and fortune triggered promiscuity. It was nice to be in the company of someone who hadn't been spoiled by success.

He stood in front of a display sent to the library by the publicity department of his publishers. There was a large posed photograph of the author looking soulful, along with a blown-up image of his bestselling book, *Stray Leaves in Autumn*. On a table beside him were stacked piles of the recently published paperback edition.

Jude was as pleased as the rest of the audience to hear the writer's words. Burton St Clair had not always been so emotionally secure. Nor indeed had he always been Burton St Clair. Jude had known him some twenty years before when he was called Al (short for Albert) Sinclair, still living in Morden with his first wife, an actress called Megan. And if marrying her had been the 'mistake' he had made when he was 'young and foolish', Jude reckoned that, during the marriage, Burton's irrepressible habit of trying to get into bed with every other woman he met had possibly been another mistake.

She had not been surprised when she heard, through mutual friends, that Al and his wife had split up after four years. Soon after they got married, Megan had gone through one of those moments in the sun which happen in actresses' careers. A supporting role in one television series had led to a starring role in another, and for a couple of years Megan Georgeson (her maiden and professional name) was everywhere on the box.

Though Al Sinclair claimed to be delighted by his wife's success, it was not an easy burden for someone as egotistical as he was. After a few experiences of accompanying her to premieres and awards ceremonies as the 'token spouse', increasingly he let her do that kind of stuff on her own. He was sick of being seated next to show-business successes and being asked the question, 'And what do you do?' To reply that he was a writer risked being asked the supplementary question, 'Do you write anything I would have heard of?' And since his first novel had yet to be published, the answer to that had to be 'No'. It was not an admission Al Sinclair enjoyed making. And he compensated for his sidelining in the marriage by various and continuing infidelities.

Megan Georgeson, dark-haired, petite and with 'surprisingly blue eyes', was often described as 'waiflike' or having 'a fragile beauty'. Unfortunately, she was equally fragile and needy in her private life. It had only been a matter of time before she found out about one – or more – of her husband's betrayals. And to someone as sensitive as Megan, such a revelation would have been a severe body blow, which the marriage could not survive.

Still, Jude was by nature a generous woman and prepared to take at face value that evening's assertion that Burton had found emotional stability with his new wife. From Jude's point of view, that was good news. It meant that, if she and Burton were ever again alone together, she wouldn't have to face the tedious necessity of deterring his wandering hands.

And she tried to banish from her mind the unworthy thought that, as again she had heard through mutual friends, this new marriage to Persephone was very new indeed. Less than six months old. There was always the possibility that Burton's old behaviours might reassert themselves. But, for the moment, she was prepared to give him the benefit of the doubt.

Time changed people, she knew, occasionally for the better. And it had been a long time since she, Burton and Megan had spent much time together.

The event was taking place in Fethering Library. Though the radiators were turned up to full, the place still felt draughty. The Edwardians who had designed its gothic dimensions must have been a hardier breed than their twenty-first century descendants, pampered from birth by central heating. Outside it was a bitterly cold January evening. A pitiless wind from the Channel assaulted the seafront of Fethering, which still called itself a village, though it had the dimensions of a small town. And the sudden rainbursts of the day, undecided whether they should be falling as snow, had compromised by turning to face-scouring sleet.

Jude had been lucky. Nothing had fallen from the sky during her half-mile walk from Woodside Cottage to the library. Optimistic by nature, she hadn't bothered to take an umbrella and, as outerwear, put on one of her favourite patchwork jackets, confident that brisk movement would keep her warm.

The route had taken her along the seafront. She had seen very few people. In the winter, when darkness fell, most of the denizens of Fethering scuttled inside and closed their curtains. As she passed by, from one of the seaside shelters, which afforded little protection because most of the glass panes in its metal structure had been smashed, she heard sounds of dispirited carousing. She could see the blurred outlines of three or four figures inside. Bored teenagers, she assumed, for whom there was not much entertainment beyond drink and drugs in a West Sussex seaside village.

Or maybe the people in the shelter could be described as – a term that was anathema to the righteous locals – 'vagrants'. The use of the word implied the unspoken qualifying adjective 'foreign'. The appearance of such people in the genteel environs of Fethering had been the cause of much apocalyptic brooding in the village's only pub, the Crown & Anchor. And had even prompted a couple of letters to the *Fethering Observer*. There was dark talk of 'slippery slopes' and 'uncontrolled immigration'.

There's a nasty substratum of racism very close to the genteel surface of the English country village. Poles, Bulgarians and Romanians are never quite welcome in the world of cricket pavilions, warm beer and roses round the door.

Jude was pretty cold by the time she reached the library and, feeling the chill once she stepped inside, wished she'd put on a more substantial top layer.

As she looked around the fine, though rather grubby, Edwardian interior, Jude felt a pang of guilt. To her shame, Fethering Library was not somewhere she visited very often. Though vaguely aware of headlines in the *Observer* about threats of the library's closure, she still tended to resort to the seductive simplicity of buying books from Amazon. She justified this to herself on the grounds that most of the books she bought, in the Mind, Body and Spirit category, were essential to her work as a healer and needed to be permanently available for reference on her shelves at Woodside Cottage. Also, she justified to herself, buying a book was putting money directly into the pocket of the author, which had to be a good thing.

But she still knew she ought to have given more support to her local library.

Her next-door neighbour Carole used to be equally absent from the place, but that had changed with the appearance of her granddaughter, Lily. As the little girl grew, her parents Stephen and Gaby – like all middle-class parents – were very keen for her to develop a love of books, and enrolled her in their local library in Fulham. So, for the precious days when Carole looked after her granddaughter in her home, High Tor, it made sense to get the little girl a ticket for Fethering Library. In order to effect this, Carole had had to get an adult ticket for herself. From then on, visits to the library could provide the focus for a major excursion, which would always end up with an ice cream or a millionaire shortbread – depending on the time of year – at the Seaview Café on Fethering Beach. (Carole would have preferred to take Lily to the rather more genteel Polly's Cake Shop, but that had closed, to be replaced by a Starbucks. And there was no way Carole Seddon was going to take her granddaughter into one of *those*.)

Jude had asked her neighbour whether she wanted to come

along with her to hear Burton St Clair's talk, but had received the predictably frosty response that Carole had better things to do with her time than 'listening to some writer moaning on about what hell it is being a writer.' Carole Seddon was wary of anything that might involve pretension or 'showing off', so treated everything to do with the creative arts with considerable suspicion. She was not a Philistine but found, now she lived in Fethering, that books and television supplied her cultural needs.

There had been a time, in the early days of her marriage to David, when the two of them had seen a lot of London theatre and cinema, but such excursions had been curtailed by the arrival of Stephen. And then things had started to go wrong between husband and wife; wrong to the extent that they put more effort into avoiding each other than arranging mutual cultural visits. And, after the divorce, Carole Seddon never again picked up the habit of theatre- and cinema-going. Not that she ever talked about such things. Even Jude, the nearest Carole had to a close friend, had never been told much about her neighbour's life before she'd moved to Fethering full time.

The relationship between Carole and Jude was a complex but enduring one. Brought together by geography when Jude moved into Woodside Cottage, next door to Carole's home High Tor, they had got off to a slow start.

Carole Seddon had always kept her life very circumscribed. She both resented and envied her new neighbour's more laid-back approach. Much more fragile than her brusque external manner might suggest, Carole was constantly anticipating disasters and very resistant to sharing her feelings with anyone. For her any activity, social or work-related, required a great deal of anguished planning. Jude was more spontaneous and, though she had not led a life free of suffering, was ready to live in the minute and embrace any opportunity which was offered. She regarded life as a rich gift. Carole thought of it more as an imposition.

Their backgrounds too couldn't have been more different. Carole had retired early – been retired early, some might say – from working as a civil servant at the Home Office. Whereas Jude, having had a portfolio of careers including model, actress and restaurateur, had ended up working as a healer. This was a calling which Carole, though she no longer expressed the opinion quite so often to her neighbour, still regarded as 'New Age mumbo-jumbo'. Illness, for her, was something that should be either snapped-out-of or dealt with by prescription medicine; she didn't think the mind had anything to do with it.

Yet somehow the relationship between the two women survived, and even mellowed. They didn't live in each other's pockets, but they saw a lot of each other. They had even gone on holiday together to Turkey. And, apart from someone out there getting murdered and Carole nearly getting murdered, that had gone pretty well.

But the experiment hadn't led to further mutual holidays. As her granddaughters, Lily and Chloe, grew older, Carole's vacations now involved entertaining them for a few days on the South Coast. Jude spent her downtime in more varied ways, and her holidays were often connected with her work. For instance, the previous summer she had spent a blissful week at a Mindfulness Workshop in Périgord. Carole's views on such activities were entirely predictable.

Yet the chalk and cheese somehow blended. And perhaps the strongest bond between Carole and Jude was their mutual passion for solving crimes.

Burton St Clair was fluent, Jude had to give him that. His presentation was clever too. It was clearly a routine he'd done many times before, but he didn't let it sound rehearsed. He stumbled over his words occasionally and every now and then went off at a tangent, as if suddenly recalling an anecdote from deep within his memory. Jude, who had sat over many a dinner table with Megan, listening to Al Sinclair before he was published, had heard most of the material before, but could not prevent herself from admiring the way he made it sound new-minted.

He certainly held the literary ladies of Fethering in the palm of his hand. They had already been predisposed towards him. Probably every one of them had read his breakthrough novel, *Stray Leaves in Autumn*, whose paperback cover was so prominently displayed on the screen behind him. Why that book had caught the *zeitgeist* in the way it had, nobody could tell. His previous eight novels had received respectable but less than ecstatic reviews, and less than respectable sales. Burton St Clair's future had appeared to be that of many other midlist authors, dutifully published by the same publishers for some years, until the inevitable moment of fate arrived. Some new broom appointed to the editorial department took a long hard look at the sales figures of his books and unceremoniously dumped him.

Burton St Clair would have coped with that. During his 'undiscovered years', he had got very good at moaning about what hell it is being a writer. Being dropped by his publisher would just have confirmed his view that the entire world was conspiring against him. Burton's shoulders were home to more chips than McDonald's.

But he was coping much more easily with being a success. Like many writers, he had spent a great deal of the unproductive times behind his desk imagining the answers he would supply when interviewed in a variety of arts programmes. So, when there was sufficient interest in *Stray Leaves in Autumn* for him actually to be interviewed on arts programmes, his replies were well rehearsed.

Quite why that particular book had taken off when the others hadn't remained a mystery. His new-broom editor, who had been about to drop him from her list, asserted that it was a vindication of the publishing house's 'long tradition of nurturing exceptional talents.' Burton himself claimed that, though no reader would ever recognize the author's 'self' in the novel, it was the book in which he had 'invested' most of himself.

It was the view of Jude, who had of course read the book, that if there was any explanation of its sudden success, it was because *Stray Leaves in Autumn* was, at its most basic, an old-fashioned romance. In spite of some stylistic embellishments and the mandatory juggling of timeframes that qualified it as 'literary fiction', the book could easily have been shortlisted for an award from the Romantic Novelists' Association.

Her own, private view was that *Stray Leaves in Autumn* was rather mawkish. While she could recognize the skill of the writing and structure, she found it horribly soft in the middle. She just hoped that, in the course of the evening ahead, Burton

wouldn't ask directly for her opinion of his novel. Jude had
never been very good at lying.

Stray Leaves in Autumn chronicled the travails of a film
director – clever that, not a writer, so that no one could ever
imagine that the central character was actually the author. His
name was Tony, which sounded nothing like Burton, and long
ago he'd been at Oxford University (totally unlike Burton, who'd
been to Cambridge). Mind you, both men, real and fictional,
were fifty-three years old.

At the beginning of the book, Tony is in the doldrums. His
career had never really taken off. He is creatively sterile and
still in mourning for his wife, Maureen, who had died two years
previously after a long battle with breast cancer. Tony's prospects
– and the possibility of happiness returning to his life – revive
when he meets Celia, a former wild child from the fringes of
the music industry who, now a divorcée in her fifties, has written
a so-far-unpublished novel, which she is convinced would
make a great movie. She is also convinced that the right person
to direct it is Tony.

Experienced readers of romance would by this point in the
book have realized that he and Celia were not only the right
people to bond creatively, but also the right people to bond
emotionally. Tony, however, proves remarkably unaware of this
blindingly obvious fact, so it is not until the couple – and the
development of their film – have endured a sequence of setbacks
and tribulations that he eventually recognizes true love. This
revelation happens, needless to say, at the premiere of the movie,
which of course goes on to be an international success.

Though Burton St Clair would never have admitted it, Jude
reckoned it was by serendipity rather than calculation that he'd
managed to press so many relevant buttons in *Stray Leaves in
Autumn*. Popular entertainment had taken a surprisingly long
time to recognize the increase in average age of the first
world's population. It kept its focus on attracting new, younger
audiences rather than catering for the growing numbers of the
robust ageing.

When a couple of successful movies and television series
featuring mature central characters woke the entertainment
moguls up to this self-evident fact, suddenly you couldn't move

for late-flowering lust: in movies, on television and in bookshops. The publication of *Stray Leaves in Autumn* fortunately coincided with this wave of geriatric romance. Rather than fulfilling his own fantasies (like most middle-aged male authors) and making the object of his hero's affections a much younger woman, Burton had been shrewd to focus Tony's interest on someone of his own age. And the fact that his novel was just an old-fashioned romance with a happy ending had been disguised by enough tricks of post-modernism and magical realism for the *literati* not to feel they were demeaning themselves by reading it.

Thinking about Burton's past had distracted Jude from listening to what he was pontificating about. She gave herself a mental rap over the knuckles and concentrated, to hear him saying, '. . . and obviously writing a book is an activity during which the author is constantly having to make moral judgements. And I am always aware of the ethical implications when I kill someone.'

TWO

The suggestion of murder got a predictable little *frisson* of indrawn breaths from the ladies of Fethering. Burton St Clair held the pause after his statement. It was clearly an effect that he had honed over many years of repetition. Then, with a wry smile, he picked up. 'I should say at this point that I never have actually killed anyone in real life, but as an author one frequently is in the godlike position of deciding whether a character should live or die. And that's a responsibility that one has to take seriously. I'm not in the business, as a *crime writer* might be—' he spoke the words with appropriate contempt – 'of killing people simply for the convenience of my plots. If a character in one of my books dies, I can assure you I have considered the termination of their life very seriously. He or she does not *deserve* to die – far from it in many cases – but they *need* to die to obey the artistic and emotional demands of the book that I am writing. I would be failing in my duty as a novelist if I did not kill them.

'I must say it's very interesting how much debate killing a character generates on social media.'

Di Thompson, the senior librarian, had made much in her introduction of the large number of followers Burton St Clair had on Facebook and Twitter. Looking at the average age of that evening's audience, Jude wondered how many of those present would have encountered him there. But, even as she had the thought, she realized she might be guilty of unthinking prejudice. Apparently quite a lot of people considerably older than she was were much involved in social media.

'For instance,' Burton continued, 'a lot of my followers have criticized me for killing off Clinton, Celia's fading rock-star husband in *Stray Leaves in Autumn*. He was a character who clearly struck a chord with many people. Struck a chord with me too. Needless to say. All of my characters strike a chord with me. If they didn't, I couldn't immerse myself so deeply in their lives during that agonizing time which covers the nativity of a work of fiction. I loved Clinton, but the dynamics of my story left me in no doubt that I had to sacrifice him to the greater good of my novel.'

There was an impressed stillness while the audience took in this act of creative magnanimity.

'And now . . .' the author broke the silence, nonchalantly picking up a copy of his novel, 'before I open up to questions from you, I would like to conclude with a reading from *Stray Leaves in Autumn*. And I think I dare mention to you now – you'll be the first people to know this – that all the Ts are not quite crossed and the Is dotted, but there is a *strong* interest from Hollywood in developing the book for a movie. Early days, of course, a lot can go wrong, but there's talk of Meryl Streep being interested in playing the part of Celia. And, as for Tony . . . well, there is *talk* . . . no, no, I don't want to tempt providence here. Let's just say there is a male actor being talked of who has an even greater profile than Meryl Streep. But . . .' he raised a finger to his lips '. . . keep it to yourselves, eh?' Knowing full well that they wouldn't.

Burton St Clair's reading, like the rest of his performance, sounded almost offhand, but again was the product of meticulous preparation.

He concluded on a funny line and, as he bowed his head, the audience's laughter melted into enthusiastic applause. While this was going on he poured more water into the glass he'd occasionally drunk from during his talk and took a long swig.

'Right,' said Burton with a self-depreciatingly boyish grin. 'Any questions?'

Jude wasn't to know, but when he'd started on his literary career, this cue had always been greeted with very English awkwardness, silence, and a lot of people concentrating on their shoes. Every author doing a library talk had experienced that aching hiatus. And it was frequently only ended by a member of staff from the library hosting the evening coming in with her own carefully prepared fall-back question.

But that was no longer the case. The Fethering librarian who had introduced Burton St Clair, Di Thompson, did not anticipate any such awkwardness. With dark hair cut so short she looked almost like a recent cancer patient, she sat serenely at the back of the audience, pleased with how well the evening she had set up was going. She knew that, since the mass explosion of book clubs, many of which were organized by librarians, such reticence about asking questions had long gone. Audiences at author events were well used to expressing their literary views, and question-asking hands shot up as soon as they were given the opportunity.

The hand which got in ahead of the others belonged to a thin, shaven-headed man in his fifties, who wore a safari jacket and combat trousers in a different camouflage pattern, above black Doc Martens. On being given the nod by the visiting author, he asked in a voice which combined lethargy and insolence in equal measure, 'Can you tell me why the photograph behind you is twenty years younger than you are?'

The expression on Burton St Clair's face suggested he was piqued. Since the publication of *Stray Leaves in Autumn* he'd become accustomed to wallowing in a warm bath of praise, so this very positive rudeness brought him up short. What's more, Jude recalled, he had always been extremely vain about his looks. When the photograph blown up behind him had been taken, Burton had had more hair, and it had been shot in such a way as to hide what deficiency there was. Since that time, more of the precious follicles had given up the ghost, and the overhead lighting of Fethering Library only accentuated the thinness on top of his cranium.

The author's preparedness for public speaking did not include a ready supply of lines to deal with hecklers, so all he said was, 'Oh, very amusing. Do we actually have any *serious* questions?'

Of the raised hands, he selected one belonging to a well-groomed woman – no, she would have thought of herself as a 'lady' – in her sixties. And with her question, normal fawning was mercifully restored.

'Mr St Clair . . .' she began.

'Call me "Burton", please.'

'Very well . . . Burton, one thing I can't help noticing in *Stray Leaves in Autumn* . . . and I've come across the same thing in your earlier books . . .' The author's good humour was instantly restored – a reader who'd read his *previous* books was clearly a serious fan '. . . is that you do have a very deep understanding of women characters, you seem to be able to get inside the female brain. Is this something that you've had to work on very hard, or is it something that just came naturally?'

'I'm very glad you asked me that question.' And he was. It gave him an unrivalled opportunity to demonstrate what an unusually sensitive man he was; to show, in fact, his feminine side. 'The thing is,' he went on, 'I do actually *like* women . . . and I'm not sure that that's a universal masculine characteristic.' His words prompted sympathetic nods and sighs of regret from his listeners. He then elaborated at some length about how much more empathetic he found female than male company. Burton St Clair drew around himself the mantle of The Perfect Man – caring, appreciative of women's contributions to life, aware of the shortcomings of his own gender, and yet safely and loyally married. The Fethering audience could not get enough of him, though Jude found herself adding liberal loads of salt to every word he spoke. She had known Al Sinclair too long to be totally taken in by Burton St Clair.

Eventually his disquisition on the natural rapport he felt with women came to an end, and he looked around for another question.

The raised hand he selected belonged to a man in his sixties, dressed in a light tweed jacket and expensively faded pinkish trousers. He had about him the ease of having been to the right schools and university.

'I was interested, Burton, in what you said about crime fiction . . .'

'Ah.' The author smiled. 'I'm not really here this evening to talk about crime fiction.'

'Perhaps not, but your comments on the subject . . .' the questioner looked down at some notes he had made '. . . when you said you were not in the business "as a *crime writer* might be – of killing people simply for the convenience of my plots".'

'And I stand by that. Though plot is a significant ingredient in any kind of story-telling, in literary fiction it does not have the primacy that it does in crime fiction.'

'Are you talking here about Golden Age crime fiction or more contemporary stuff?'

'Does it make much difference?' asked Burton St Clair loftily.

'Oh, so you're saying all crime fiction is an inferior genre?'

'I'm not saying "inferior",' said Burton, though he clearly was. 'I'm sure there's some very fine writing in the crime world, but I just feel that, for me, the crime novel would not offer sufficient space to explore the ideas that I need to pursue in my own work.'

'Hm,' said the man with the pink trousers. 'There is of course quite a history of *literary novelists* . . .' The way he spoke the words implied a level of pretension within the breed '. . . sneering at the works of—'

'I'm not sneering. Far be it from me to—'

'John Banville, for instance,' his interlocutor went on implacably, 'is well known for writing his crime novels as Benjamin Black and referring to them as "cheap fiction", when compared to his literary novels. And the CV of Booker Prize-winning Julian Barnes doesn't draw attention to the Duffy novels he published under the name of Dan Kavan—'

'I don't think any of this is really relevant to this evening's discussion.'

'Oh, but it is,' the questioner persisted. His manner was not aggressive, it was infinitely reasonable. He argued with the skill of an experienced debater, someone who had always dealt with words. 'We're here to talk about your work and I am particularly interested in the books published – self-published – under the name of Seth Marston which—'

Burton St Clair was clearly rattled now. 'I'm going to have to cut you off there,' he interrupted.

'Are you saying you don't know the works of Seth Marston?'

'I've never heard the name. We're here this evening to talk about my novel *Stray Leaves in Autumn*.' The author appealed to his audience. 'Do we have another question *on that subject*?'

The woman whose raised hand was favoured this time was inordinately tall and expensively blonde, dressed in a slightly fussy pink jacket over an extremely fussy cream blouse. 'I don't think we should leave the subject of mystery fiction.' Her voice had the relaxed refinement of an East Coast American intellectual. 'The gentleman who spoke before mentioned the Golden Age, and that is a topic on which I have done considerable research, and indeed on which I teach a college course. I'm very interested in the relationship between classic mystery fiction and its so-called "literary" counterparts. I wondered if you, as a—'

'I'm sorry to interrupt you there,' said Burton St Clair, who clearly wasn't sorry at all, 'but without wishing to sound egotistical, I thought this evening we were meant to be talking about *my* books rather than those of the Golden Age, however *classic* they may be.' Quickly, before the American could come back at him, he pleaded, 'Now do we have another *relevant* question?'

One of his worshipful company of ladies came to the rescue. 'From my reading of *Stray Leaves in Autumn*, I get the impression that you believe some level of adversity actually strengthens the bonds of love. Is that true?'

'Oh yes, certainly. And it's very perceptive of you to pick up on that. Shakespeare tells us "the course of true love never did run smooth", and I think that there, as in many other areas of life, experience – and not always happy experience – can intensify the emotional reaction to . . .'

And Burton St Clair was off again, laying bare the depths of his sincerity to the good people of Fethering.

Jude was less convinced by his oratory than most of them. She remembered Megan telling her that, in his years as an aspiring but rejected writer, Al Sinclair had scraped up enough money to have three crime novels vanity-published. She didn't know that they'd been written under the name of Seth Marston, but it wouldn't have surprised her. It would have been in character for Burton St Clair to have lied about his early history as a writer.

THREE

Tickets for the Burton St Clair Author evening had cost five pounds, but that included a glass of wine. So as soon as she had finished her speech of thanks to the author, Di Thompson busied herself and her helpers with moving the furniture to make room for the less formal part of the evening. There was limited space in Fethering Library and the drink-dispensing table could not be set up until the chairs had been folded away.

Most of the audience stood patiently while this process took place. A few public-spirited souls helped with the chair-folding. Maybe they were just being helpful, or perhaps volunteers had been delegated to the task. There was a purpose-built trolley with prongs on to which the chairs had to be hung. Jude noticed that the man in pink trousers was one of those doing his duty. The more infirm audience members stayed resolutely in place. They were not going to risk losing their chairs.

One elderly woman, in a trouser suit from a different era, was doughtily helping, however. Though it looked as if she needed the chair she was moving to support her frail body. Jude moved forward to assist.

'It's all right,' said the woman in a reedy but cultured voice. 'I can manage.'

'Well, if you're sure . . .'

'Oh yes. I've been moving chairs at this library since long before you moved here, Jude.'

She was unsurprised that the woman knew her name. Even if they'd never actually met, most residents of Fethering knew the names and personal histories (true and embellished) of everyone else in the village. 'I'm sorry, I've seen you around, but I don't know your name.'

'Eveline Ollerenshaw, but everyone calls me "Evvie".' It was clear she regarded this conversational opening as an opportunity for a break in her strenuous task. Propping herself up on the chair, she continued, 'I live right next door to the library.' She gestured through the wall. 'Been here since I moved down when my husband Gerald retired, and he passed on in 1997. I've been volunteering here ever since then. I do love books, you see. They've been such a comfort to me. I was a volunteer here before Di Thompson took over. She often says she couldn't manage without me.'

Jude recognized the type, the woman whose motive for offering her services as a volunteer was loneliness. Evvie worked at Fethering Library because it offered her the opportunity to talk to people. She probably was useful at times, but as she grew older became more of a liability. People like Evvie would create a problem for someone in Di Thompson's position. At some point, she would have to suggest that the woman's infirmity meant that her helpful volunteering days were over. Yet she would know that, when she spoke those words, she would be destroying what remained of the woman's life. And, since Eveline Ollerenshaw lived right next door to the library, the old lady would be constantly reminded of what she had lost.

Jude saw this all in a flash, and what happened next illustrated the situation perfectly. The chair Evvie leant on in the middle of the room was now the only one unstacked. Di Thompson came across, saying, 'Can I give you a hand with that?'

'No, I can manage,' the old lady repeated with dignity. And, dragging the chair behind her, she tottered across towards the trolley.

Jude took advantage of the lull to find the Ladies. It was through the staff room which, compared to the chilly space of the main library, was almost excessively hot.

Jude was not to know it, but a library staff room would have been a very familiar sight to Burton St Clair – or indeed any other author. A career in literature involves many library talks and, before each one, the staff room is where the visiting writer is invariably ensconced. There he or she will be offered sandwiches, cakes and something to drink. This last may sometimes be a glass of wine. More often it's tea or coffee and, occasionally, the minimum hospitality of a glass of water.

Conversation would be manufactured during this pre-talk hiatus by a senior librarian, who would keep having to rush off to check that the chairs are set out properly or that relevant volunteers have arrived and know what to do. The librarian might also double-check with the author the text of the introduction that she (it usually is a she) is planning to make. She is almost always more nervous about delivering these two minutes than the writer is about spouting for the three-quarters of an hour of all the old rubbish that he or she has delivered many times before.

The staff room of Fethering Library was almost identical to all the others around the country. There was a sink, over which hung a row of mugs (whose ownership was a carefully respected issue of protocol). There was a fridge, and lockers in which the staff would stow their valuables. Shelves were piled with books and files. Pinned on a corkboard were various directives from the county librarian, mostly about Health & Safety issues. There was also literature from Unison, the public service users' union.

Under a table was a cardboard box on which was written in blue felt pen: 'JAM JARS FOR VERONICA'.

Three bottles of red wine stood on the work surface. Their screw-tops had not been unscrewed. Being allowed to 'breathe' would not have made much difference to wine of that quality. Presumably the white was still in the fridge beneath.

On her return journey from the Ladies, Jude noticed that the wine bottles were still there. And, back in the main library space, she found their delayed appearance was causing complaint.

'Come on, we're meant to be getting a drink! Speed it up a bit! There are people dying of alcohol deprivation out here!'

The shouts came from the man who had had a go at Burton

St Clair about his photograph. Clearly, he had a habit of bad manners. The good ladies of Fethering moved a little further away from him and, once space had been cleared, they clustered round the table where Burton St Clair was signing paperbacks of *Stray Leaves in Autumn*. As well as setting up the display screens, his publishers had also arranged a healthy supply of the books. They clearly regarded this particular author as one to invest in. And the way copies were being snatched up suggested that their instincts were correct.

Because most of the audience was preoccupied with the evening's author, Jude found herself one of the first in the queue once the drinks table had finally been set up. The only person ahead of her was, predictably enough, the man in camouflage kit. A junior member of the library staff, a dumpy girl with green-dyed hair and too many facial piercings, was rather shakily pouring white wine into lines of glasses.

'You got any red?' asked the man.

'Yes, I was just about to pour—'

'Well, move it along, darling. I'm panting for a glass of red.'

The girl fumbled with opening the relevant bottle. Thank goodness it was a screw-top; dealing with a corkscrew might have been beyond her. As soon as she had poured one glass, camouflage man had picked it up and downed the contents in one. Then he held the glass out for a refill.

The junior librarian looked confused. She must have been instructed that the five-pound admission charge only included one glass of wine, but she was too cowed by the man's bellig-erence to argue with him. Her expression also suggested that she wasn't too bothered. The girl carried with her an air of truculent boredom. She refilled his glass.

'Thanks, sweetie,' he said, and moved away from the table with the satisfaction of someone who'd proved a point. Jude picked up a glass of white and followed him.

'I was interested in what you said about the photograph,' she lied. But she did want to get into conversation with this man. Her work as a healer had increased her natural curiosity about human psychology, and the man's behaviour had intrigued her. Immediate confrontational rudeness of the kind he had just demonstrated did not come from nowhere.

Before he'd had time to respond to her opening remark, she thrust out a hand to him. 'I'm Jude.'

He only hesitated for a moment before taking it and squeezing with a little more pressure than was necessary. Close to, he looked more youthful, early forties perhaps. A decade younger than she was.

'Steve Chasen,' he said. Jude recognized from long familiarity the way he was appraising her. She had always been attractive to men and, even now when her body had filled out and the haystack of hair on top of her head might no longer be naturally blonde, the magnetism remained. It did not worry her. She was not offended by men's interest. And, though she never exploited it, she recognized that her attractiveness could sometimes be useful.

'Well, it was a bit ridiculous, wasn't it?' said Steve Chasen. 'With the real him bald in front of that poncy image that looks like a bloody album cover.'

'Publicity photographs,' Jude observed, 'have always been more touched up than air hostesses.'

He conceded her a giggle.

'And are you a writer?' she asked. It was an educated guess. Why else would he be at the library to insult another author?

'Yes,' he replied, with a glint of hope in his eyes. 'Have you read any of my stuff?'

Jude was forced to admit that she hadn't.

'You and a few billion others,' he said cynically.

'What sort of books do you write?'

'Bloody good ones.' He curled his lip. 'Not that any publishers have yet recognized that fact.'

'Ah. So you never have been published?'

He raised an admonitory finger and shook it at her. 'Ah, depends what you mean by "published". Not so easy to define these days. There are more possibilities out there than chopping down trees to produce *Stray Leaves in Autumn*.' He gestured with contempt towards the table where Burton was still signing, full of bonhomie and magnanimity. 'My books may not be "published" in the traditional sense, but they're out there.'

'By "out there" do you mean they're e-books?'

'Better than that. You can read them online, through my website. And I've got links to them through social media.'

Jude nodded, thinking that it had never been easier for a writer to make his book available, but the old problem remained. How did you get potential readers to *know* that it was available? The established publishing houses with their publicity departments would always have the advantage over the individual, self-promoting author.

She found that a cheaply printed garish flyer had been thrust into her hand. *Revenge of the Plague Planet* was the book it touted. How had she known from the start that Steve Chasen would write science fiction? Though she read little fiction of any kind (except when she was on holiday), Jude had always had a strong resistance to anything involving other worlds or aliens. Through her varied life, she had encountered as much weirdness as she needed to in the real world.

'You'll like it,' the author assured her. 'Really got some ideas in it. Makes you think. Not like that bland pap which people like *him* produce.' There was another derisory gesture made in the direction of Burton St Clair.

'Do you actually know Burton?' asked Jude.

'What if I do?' came the defensive reply.

'Nothing, really. I just wondered what he'd done to annoy you.'

'People like that don't need to do anything to annoy me. His very existence annoys me. The world would be a better place if Burton St Clair wasn't in it!' Apparently deciding that he wasn't going to better this as an exit line, Steve Chasen moved abruptly away from Jude. Saying, 'I'm going to get another refill,' he went across to cause further embarrassment to the young librarian at the drinks table.

'Bit old to play the *enfant terrible* card, isn't he?'

Jude turned at the sound of this urbane voice and found herself facing the man in pink trousers. Because her previous vantage point had been from behind the rows of chairs, this was the first time she'd seen him from the front. He was probably in his sixties, but he wore it well. His hair, ringing a central bald patch, was long but well cut. His generous lips wore a pleasingly sardonic expression.

'I'm talking about God's gift to the world of science fiction,' he continued, nodding in the direction in which Steve Chasen had gone.

'I thought you must be. So I gather you know him?'

'Met him when the library set up a Writers' Group. He was a member for a while; stopped coming when he discovered that other people wanted to talk about their writing too.'

'Ah. Does that mean you're a writer?'

'Hardly. Spent my working life dealing with scripts, though.' Jude looked at him for an explanation. 'Television director. No work now, I'm afraid. Producers tend to favour the younger model.'

'So you joined the Writers' Group because you wanted to try your hand at creating your own television scripts?'

'Good Lord, no. If there's ageism in directing, there's even more in writing. With a couple of famous exceptions, no one over sixty gets a look-in. Over fifty, probably. Television is a young man's game.' He spoke wryly, but without bitterness. He was just accepting the way the entertainment business worked.

'If you're not writing scripts in the Writers' Group, what do you write?'

'Very little. Or, to be more accurate, nothing. I went to a few meetings, but it wasn't really for me. Full of old biddies who thought they could write poetry. Though actually I should be careful who I describe as "old biddies". In this day and age, the phrase is no doubt sexist. What's more, the people I'm referring to are probably the same age as I am.'

'Is it the Writers' Group who organized this evening with Al . . . Burton?' asked Jude.

'No, that's the library staff. The Writers' Group actually no longer exists. Apparently, got too expensive. Funding cuts, you know, hitting libraries hard. Places like this have to rely increasingly on volunteers.'

'Like you?'

'What do you mean?'

'I saw you dutifully folding up chairs.'

'Yes, and I came early to put them out too. Least one can do. Anyway, I think, once they couldn't use the library, the Writers' Group started meeting in people's houses. Whether they still do, I don't know. I rather lost interest. But the former members certainly knew all about this evening.' He looked round. 'There are a lot of them here.' He focused his attention back on Jude. 'You called him "Burton". Does that mean you know him?'

'I was a friend of his first wife. Used to see a lot of them at one point. We're talking twenty years ago. I haven't seen either of them for a while.'

'Well, I wouldn't think he needs other female friends now he's got the immaculate Persephone.' The man spoke with sly cynicism, and his words ambiguously contained the possibility that Jude's relationship with the author might have been more than friendly.

Jude instantly picked up on that. 'As I said, it was Megan who was my friend. I only met Burton through her.'

'And are you saying he never came on to you?'

'No, I'm saying that when he did come on to me, I gave him a very immediate and firm brush-off.'

'Hm.'

'The way you talk about him . . . I'm sorry, I don't know your name . . .?'

'Oliver. Oliver Parsons.'

'I'm Jude.'

'Yes, I know.'

'Oh?'

'Come on, we both live in Fethering. Almost everyone in the place knows the names of all the others, even if they've never actually met.'

'True. So I'm surprised I don't know yours. And surprised we haven't met before. Or even seen you round the place before.'

'I used to travel a lot when I was directing. And now maybe I keep myself to myself. My wife died a couple of years back. I think she must have been the social one in our partnership.'

'Oh, I'm sorry.'

He shrugged. 'One recovers.'

'Anyway, what I was going to say, Oliver, is that the way you talk about him, it sounds as if you know Burton.'

'I don't *know* him, but I know a lot about him.'

'Oh?'

But he didn't take the cue to open up as much as Jude had hoped. 'As you may have gathered from my questions,' he said, 'I'm very interested in crime fiction.'

'Yes.' Jude didn't feel inclined to admit at that moment what she knew about Burton's earlier writing, probably under the pseudonym of Seth Marston. She still had some residual loyalty to him. She'd wait and see where Oliver Parsons was going with the subject.

'I've made a bit of a study of the Golden Age,' he went on. 'You know, Twenties, Thirties . . .'

'Christie, Sayers, that lot . . .'

'Exactly. And some of the less well-known ones. Yes, I got quite caught up in it, the research and so on, at the start. Some of the murder methods and things are quite ingenious, but . . .' The tailing-off of his words suggested that the appeal of the Golden Age was fading for him.

At this moment, further conversation was prevented by the arrival of Di Thompson, who had just emerged from the staff room, clutching a sheaf of printed sheets. 'Sorry, forgot these,' she said in a rather flustered manner. 'Evaluation forms. If you could just fill them in to say what you thought of the evening . . .?'

'Are we allowed to be honest?' asked Oliver Parsons sardonically.

'Well, of course,' Di replied, clearly not skilled in picking up when someone was joking. 'That's the aim of the exercise. If you need a pen, Vix has got some over at the drinks table.'

'No, it's fine, I've got one.' Oliver reached into his tweed jacket.

The just-mentioned Vix was now sidling over, trying to attract her superior's attention. Jude noticed that, as well as the green hair and piercings, a red snake tattoo was crawling up the girl's neck. Her voice was local West Sussex, whiny and slightly put-upon. 'Di, don't know what I should do. There's this feller who keeps just filling up his wine glass and they're only supposed to get one—'

'I can't be bothered with that now, I'm busy!'

The sharpness of the reaction surprised Jude. When she had introduced Burton at the beginning and then thanked him at the end, Di Thompson had seemed a mild, rather benign personality, but her mood had certainly changed. Or maybe Vix, the junior librarian, had always got on her boss's nerves. There was a recalcitrance about the girl's body language which suggested she might not be the easiest person in the world to work with.

But even as Jude had this thought, another explanation offered itself. The star of the evening, Burton St Clair, came out from the same door as Di and, as he insinuated his arm around her waist, said, 'Well, how about a drink for me? I think I've deserved one.'

The way the librarian flinched, and the speed with which she disconnected herself, asking a sharp 'Red or white?', suggested that, however well he'd gone down with most of his female audience, here was one Fethering woman Burton St Clair had failed to charm.

FOUR

B urton St Clair asked for red wine and there was a moment of confusion while Vix Winter explained to her senior that there wasn't any left on her table and she'd have to go back to the staff room to get some. Di, apparently unwilling to spend more time with the evening's guest than she had to, said she'd come and help.

Burton St Clair directed at Jude what he would probably have defined as 'a roguish smile'. 'Long time no see. I'm so glad you made the effort to come to hear my modest presentation.'

'No worries. I live just down the road.'

'Funny. When we used to see a lot of each other, in what feels like another life, it never occurred to me you might end up in a backwater like Fethering.'

Jude shrugged. 'It suits me very well.'

'And what are you doing now? When we last met you were a restaurateur . . . or was it a model?'

'I did a bit of both back then.'

'And are you still . . .?'

His look suggested that Jude's fuller figure might not now

be so much in demand for fashion shoots. Rather than be offended by the implication, she giggled. 'I've done a lot of things since then. Now I'm a healer.'

'A healer?' Burton's eyebrows rose towards his receding hairline. 'What, you mean "laying on of hands" and ginseng and bloody dumping hot stones on people's—'

Fortunately, before she had time to defend her profession against this predictable flood of scepticism, their conversation was interrupted by the opening of the door to the staff room. An unwilling Steve Chasen was the first to emerge, being pushed out by Di Thompson.

'It wasn't my bloody fault!' he was protesting. 'I didn't spill it!'

'Yes, you did,' countered the librarian. 'And you shouldn't have been in there, anyway. The staff—'

'You pushed the bottle over! I saw you!' said Steve Chasen.

'Do you need a hand?' interposed the urbane voice of Oliver Parsons.

Di Thompson looked gratefully at her saviour, as Oliver took over her pushing duties. 'Come on, old chap. You've just had a little bit too much to drink and I think it'd be better if—'

'I'm going!' said Steve Chasen, shaking himself free of his latest ejector and turning to face Burton St Clair. 'I don't want to stay in the same room as a bloody liar like you!' He shook a finger at the more successful author. 'But don't worry, you'll get your comeuppance!'

Then, with a failed attempt at dignity, Steve Chasen staggered out of the library.

Burton chose to ignore the interruption and, with a smiling face, turned towards the staff-room door, from which Vix Winter was issuing with his long-awaited glass of wine. She too was serenely pretending the recent scene hadn't happened, but, as the girl passed, Jude heard her whisper to Di Thompson, 'I'll clear it up.'

'Thanks,' her superior hissed back. 'Thank God we haven't got a carpet in there.'

And Vix Winter scuttled through into the staff room.

'Anyway, cheers!' Burton St Clair raised his glass to Di. 'Many thanks for making me so welcome in Fethering Library.'

He sounded sincere, but Jude knew him well enough to know just how patronizing he was being. 'Never forget the little people' – that's what his mind was saying.

'I think maybe we should call it a day,' said Di Thompson. It was nearly half an hour later and she looked exhausted. The evening had gone on longer than expected and she had the demeanour of someone who desperately wanted to get home. Through the library windows, a sheet of sudden rain was illuminated by the moonlight.

'Yes,' said Jude. By then most of the audience had melted away. The only others still there were Burton, Di and Vix. The junior librarian was looking even more keen to get away than her boss, but apparently Di was going to give her a lift home, so she had no alternative but to wait.

'How long will it take you to drive back to London?' asked Di pointedly.

'Oh, hour and a half I should think, this time of night. Fortunately, Barnes is on the right side of the river. And the Beamer can really open up on the A3.'

Jude didn't think it was worth pointing out that Burton had had far too much wine to drive safely, since he was clearly going to do it anyway. He had form on the drinking. She remembered from way back that he always had a hipflask of whisky about his person or in the glove compartment of his car. Defiantly, at the end of a boozy evening, he would take a swig from it before driving home. She wondered whether he still did that, or had life with the saintly Persephone cured him of such antisocial habits?

She also found it interesting that the financial rewards of bestsellerdom had allowed him to graduate from Morden to the much more fashionable Barnes (and to graduate from Vauxhalls to BMWs). 'Well, it's very good to see you again,' she said. 'And I look forward to meeting Persephone at some point.'

He didn't respond to that suggestion. Instead, he asked, 'How're you getting back home?'

'Walk. It's only half a mile.'

He looked through the window. 'In this lot?'

'Won't take long.'

'Have you got an umbrella? Or a waterproof?'

'No, but—'

'Apart from the rain, it's bloody cold out there. I'll give you a lift in the Beamer.' He seemed very keen to mention his car. Maybe it was a new toy.

'Well, that sounds fine,' said Di Thompson, whose body language was urging them towards the door. 'Now if we could . . .'

Yes, the car was a new toy. Even in the face of horizontal icy rain, Burton St Clair could not help taking an appreciative look at its sleek lines before zapping the unlock button.

Judé, protected only by her patchwork jacket, needed no invitation to leap in through the passenger door. The seat where she found herself was reassuringly plush in its leather upholstery, and the interior was redolent of that 'new car' smell.

'So you live right here in Fethering?' asked Burton as he closed his door. The howling of the wind and rain dropped in volume. When he turned the ignition key, cool jazz filled the space around them.

'Yes,' she replied. 'It's not far. I'll give you directions.'

'With you, Jude, I don't need any directions.'

His left arm was suddenly around her shoulders. His right had found its way under the jacket to her breasts.

'God, Jude, how I've longed to do this,' he murmured as he pressed his face forward towards hers. 'It was agony for me every time I was with you and Megan, because you were the one I really fancied and—'

Fortunately, Jude had not had time to do up her seatbelt, which meant that her left hand was free to administer a stinging slap to Burton's cheek.

'What was that for?' he asked, aggrieved. 'Don't play hard to get. You know you've always fancied me.'

'Really? What the hell are you playing at, Al? You've just told your entire audience how perfect your life is with the sainted Persephone and now—'

'Ah, Persephone understands.'

'Does she?'

'Yes, she knows I have a more powerful sex drive than she

does; she understands that I'm attractive to other women. She wouldn't make any fuss about—'

'She might not make any fuss, but I would! And if you think, just because you've got a book in the bestseller list, that gives you some kind of *droit de seigneur* over any woman who you—'

'Come on, Jude, be grown-up! You know you've always fancied me.'

'I know many things,' she responded, with uncharacteristic hauteur. 'That I fancy you is not among them!'

She found the door handle and let herself out into the maelstrom of wind and rain. 'Goodbye, Al,' she said. 'You get back home to Persephone.'

She slammed the door of his 'Beamer' and set off resolutely towards the seafront. Long before she reached it, the rain had seeped through her patchwork jacket and was trickling down her back and between her breasts. The cold penetrated to the very core of her being.

Before going left along the promenade, Jude turned back to look at Fethering Library. The BMW was still where it was when she had left it, with no exterior or interior lights on. As she turned towards the sea, there was no sign of activity from the glass-shattered shelter.

By the time she got back to Woodside Cottage, she was in desperate need of a hot shower to bring some warmth back into her frozen body.

She also needed the shower because she felt soiled by her encounter with Burton St Clair's wandering hands.

FIVE

After the shower, Jude still felt restless and wakeful. Uncharacteristically, she poured herself a large Scotch and took it to bed with her laptop. To her surprise, she found she still had Megan Sinclair's email address. There'd been no contact between them for more than fifteen years. Quite possibly Megan's email had changed in that time, but, though she wasn't about to write, 'Your ex-husband came on to me this evening', Jude did feel the need to be in touch with her old friend.

They had been very close at one time, even talked of sharing a flat together, though that never happened. But as girls to giggle with and shoulders to cry on, they had supported each other through a variety of dating disasters and false dawns of love. Jude felt confident that, if they did meet, the old rapport would be quickly re-established.

The email message she composed ran: 'Seeing Al strutting his stuff in our local library this evening made me think about you. And when I say "local", perhaps I should point out that I'm now living on the South Coast not far from Worthing in a village called Fethering. No idea where you are – still Morden? – or indeed what's happening in your life. Be nice to meet and catch up some time. Oh, and by the way, when Al self-published those early books, did he use the pseudonym "Seth Marston"? Love, Jude.'

She swallowed down the remains of the Scotch, switched off the light and, after about an hour, sank into a troubled sleep.

The next morning, when Carole came round to Woodside Cottage for coffee, Jude didn't mention the unpleasant ending to her evening at the library. She had found in the years of their acquaintance that her neighbour was inhibited in talking about sex. And for Jude to have raised the subject, even after such an unwelcome and unpleasant encounter as the night before's, would have made Carole think she was boasting about her comparative attractiveness. Jude, in Carole's view, was the kind of woman men came on to. She herself wasn't.

So Jude, sitting in the throw-covered clutter of her sitting room, let Carole initiate the conversation, which that morning – as on many other mornings – centred on the doings of her granddaughters. 'Gaby and Stephen are getting really worried about schools for Lily.'

'Surely they don't have to think about that for a couple of years.'

'Oh, but they do. Living where they are – in Fulham – you have to think a long way ahead. They've got to get Lily into the right nursery to ensure that she goes to the right junior school, because a lot of those are feeders if they want to get into somewhere really good for the next stage – and obviously that's what's really important.'

'Are we talking state education here?' asked Jude, only for the benefit of the reaction she knew she'd get.

Which duly arrived. 'Good heavens, no!' screeched Carole. 'State education is a very dangerous course to embark on if you live in London. State secondary schools are full of drugs and violence and teenage pregnancies. The thought of either of my two granddaughters going to a place like—'

The diatribe might have continued for some time, had it not been interrupted by the ringing of Jude's doorbell.

When she opened her front door and felt the clutch of cold air, she found herself confronted by two people. The woman was dressed in a smart trouser suit, the man more casual in a red zip-up fleece. The woman was carrying a large-screened iPhone. Behind them in the street was parked a police Panda car.

'Good morning,' said the woman. 'Are you Jude Nicholls?'

'Yes.'

'I'm Detective Inspector Rollins, and this is Detective Sergeant Knight. We would like to talk to you about the death of Burton St Clair.'

SIX

Though she was being interviewed in her own home (Carole had conveniently remembered something she had to do back at High Tor), Jude was left in no doubt that her police interrogation was a serious matter.

Once they were seated on the sagging, throw-covered sofa and armchairs of her sitting room, the first thing Detective Inspector Rollins said was, 'You reacted with surprise, Mrs Nicholls, when—'

'Call me "Jude". Everyone calls me "Jude".'

A slight wrinkle of the woman's nose showed that she didn't warm to such intimacy, but all she said was, 'Very well, Jude. You reacted with surprise when I mentioned Burton St Clair's death. Does that mean you didn't know he was dead?'

'Of course that's what it means!' The delayed shock of the news suddenly caught up with her. 'But I can't believe that Al . . . Burton's dead. I was with him only yesterday evening.'

'We know you were,' said Rollins. 'And we think it's possible that you were the last person to see him alive.'

'Which is why we're talking to you,' added Detective Sergeant Knight, perhaps unnecessarily. Through the confusion of her thoughts, Jude got the impression that the junior officer needed to assert himself, to demonstrate that he wasn't just a weak male sidekick to a female boss.

'Did Burton die at home?' asked Jude. 'He was about to drive there when I left him.'

'No,' the Detective Inspector replied. 'His body was found in his car this morning in the Fethering Library car park.'

Jude was bewildered. 'But that's where I last saw him.'

'Yes,' Rollins confirmed.

'Which is also why we're talking to you.' This second intervention by Knight prompted the tiniest wrinkling of his superior's brow. He had overstepped some mark in their professional relationship. The Detective Inspector's iPhone lay on her lap. Jude assumed it might contain notes about the beginning of their investigation, but Rollins gave no sign that she would be writing anything down during their interview.

'Well, how did he die?' asked Jude. 'What did he die of?'

'We don't know yet,' replied the Detective Inspector, all police formality. 'We will have more information when a post-mortem has been conducted.'

'And forensic investigations,' Knight contributed.

This again prompted a *moue* of annoyance from Rollins. Jude thought she knew why, as she asked the obvious question. 'Forensic? Does that mean there's a suspicion of foul play?'

'We're at a very early stage of our enquiries. At this point any suggestions as to the cause of Mr St Clair's death would be nothing more than speculation.'

Jude felt appropriately deterred from asking further questions.

The ball was still in the Detective Inspector's court. 'But, obviously, Jude, we are trying to get as exact a picture as we can of his movements during the last twenty-four hours. We've spoken to his wife . . .'

'And to his ex-wife?'

'Yes, we know he was married twice.' Rollins's tone was testy, as though Jude had been picking her up on some lapse in her investigative method. 'We've left a message with Megan Sinclair, as she still calls herself, but she hasn't got back to us yet.'

'Ah.'

'One of her neighbours,' Knight contributed, 'believes she's visiting an actress friend in Scarborough.'

Again, Detective Inspector Rollins's expression suggested that her junior's intervention was unwelcome. She turned back to her interviewee. 'Persephone St Clair, the deceased's widow, said you used to spend a lot of time with him and his former wife . . .?'

'Yes, there was a stage when we used to see quite a lot of each other. We're talking some years ago.'

'How many years?'

'Fifteen . . . twenty . . .'

Detective Sergeant Knight thought he had been silent for too long. 'And, back then, were you close to Mr St Clair?'

Again, Rollins looked peeved by the intervention. Maybe that was the very question she had been about to ask.

'I knew Megan before I knew him. She was my friend. When she got married, it was natural that I met up with them as a couple.'

'But as you got to know him,' Knight persisted, 'did you become closer to Mr St Clair?'

'If you're asking if we had an affair, the answer is very definitely no.'

'That wasn't what the Sergeant was asking,' said Rollins in a manner that was definitely a put-down to him. 'We are merely trying to get as much background to the case as we can.'

'"Case"?' echoed Jude. 'Then you do think there was something suspicious about—'

'I was guilty of using the wrong word,' responded the

Detective Inspector blandly. 'I should not have said "case", I should have said "incident".'

'I see.'

'So. Background,' Rollins went on. 'Had you kept in touch with Burton St Clair since the days when you spent time with him and his wife . . . some fifteen or twenty years ago?' The way she echoed the words seemed to carry the implication that Jude was not necessarily a very reliable witness.

'No, not really.'

'What do you mean by that?'

'I mean that I haven't been regularly in touch with him. I heard a bit about what he was up to from mutual friends . . .'

'Did you know that his first marriage had broken down?' asked Detective Sergeant Knight.

'I heard about that, yes. Then, obviously, I saw media coverage of the success of *Stray Leaves in Autumn* . . .'

Rollins picked up the conversational baton. 'And was that why you decided you would go and hear him speaking last night at Fethering Library? You saw in the local paper that he would be there and you thought you'd go and re-establish contact with an old friend?'

'It wasn't exactly like that.'

'Oh?' The Detective Inspector's manner made it very difficult for Jude not to sound guilty. Though, of course, she told herself, there was nothing that she needed to sound guilty for.

'Burton contacted me, said he'd be in Fethering, and suggested I might like to come along to the library.'

'So you *had* kept in regular touch?' said Detective Sergeant Knight accusingly.

'No. He contacted me through Facebook. I don't use it a lot, but I do have an account. For some of my clients it's their preferred means of communication.'

'Clients?' Rollins reminded herself. 'Oh yes, of course. You're a *healer*, aren't you?'

Jude was well used to the layers of scepticism that could be lathered on to that particular word. 'Yes, that's what I do.'

'So . . . until this approach through Facebook, you hadn't had direct contact from either Burton or his first wife Megan for fifteen . . . twenty years . . .?'

'No.'

'And you hadn't made contact with them?'

'No.' Jude suddenly remembered the previous evening. 'Well, that is to say . . .'

'Yes?'

'I did send an email to Megan yesterday.'

'Oh?' Detective Inspector Rollins's tone made this sound like a major revelation. 'Was that after you had left Fethering Library?'

'Yes, when I got back here.'

'And why, after this long break, did you suddenly get in touch with her?'

'There was a query about Burton St Clair's writing that was raised in the Q & A session after his talk. I wanted to check a factual detail with Megan.'

'I see. Well, we'll be able to see her emails when we get in touch with her.'

'I can show you the text of what I sent right now,' said Jude, as near to being rattled as her habitually serene temperament allowed.

'That won't be necessary,' said Detective Inspector Rollins. For the first time, she looked down at her iPhone, woke up the screen and consulted some notes she had written there. 'Now, according to Vix Winter, the junior librarian who found Mr St Clair's body in the car park this morning, last night, just as she and her boss were leaving, she saw you getting into Mr St Clair's car. She also said that, by then, all of the other people who'd attended the talk had gone home.'

'Yes. That's what happened. It was pouring with rain. Burton had offered to drive me back here.'

'But he didn't drive you back here. The dry patch under his car suggested that it hadn't moved since he arrived at the library earlier in the evening.'

'That's entirely possible, yes.'

'So why didn't he drive you home, Jude?'

'We had an argument.'

'Did you?'

'Yes.'

'And could you tell me what that argument was about?'

'Very well.'

'In fact, could you tell me exactly what happened last night, from the moment—' Rollins looked down at her screen to check the name – 'Di Thompson locked up the library and left in her car with Vix Winter, until you left Burton St Clair in his car . . . assuming that *is* what happened?'

The level of scepticism in the Detective Inspector's attitude and body language did not lessen as Jude began her narrative. If anything, it increased.

Jude was punctiliously accurate in her reconstruction of the events inside Burton's BMW. They were so recent that she didn't have to dig too deep into her memory. But as she replayed the awkwardness of the encounter, she was annoyed to find herself blushing. And at the end of her narration, she could sense that Rollins did not believe the truth she had just been told.

Before the Detective Inspector could pass any comment, however, the iPhone on her lap rang. 'Rollins,' she said. 'Ah, Megan Sinclair. Thank you for getting back to me.'

She rose to her feet. 'I'll take this in the hall,' she announced as she left the room.

Detective Sergeant Knight and Jude looked at each other. Neither had much to say. The silence felt heavy between them.

SEVEN

Burton St Clair's death was reported on Radio 4's *World at One*. It was the last item on the bulletin – one of the 'and we've just had a report that . . .' ones – so no details were supplied. Nor was there any trailer to say that his work and legacy would be discussed on the evening's arts programme *Front Row*. Burton himself would no doubt have reckoned he deserved such a tribute. The producers maybe did not think that one successful novel qualified him for that kind of accolade.

All the one o'clock news report did say was that he had been found dead in his car in Fethering, 'a village on the South Coast, whose library he had been visiting.'

Jude listened to the bulletin in the irreproachably tidy environs of High Tor's kitchen. Carole had rung – characteristically, rather than going next door in person – as soon as the Panda car had departed, and invited her neighbour for lunch.

The cottage cheese salad that Carole produced did not really qualify under Jude's description of 'lunch', but she was far too polite to mention the fact. Anyway, she was in no state to be assertive. The shock of Burton's death, followed so quickly by the interview with the two mistrustful detectives, had shaken Jude's customary equilibrium.

She felt vulnerable and, in spite of Carole's assiduous probing, was unwilling to divulge what had been said that morning in the sitting room of Woodside Cottage. After dutifully consuming her cottage cheese salad, she announced that she would go back home to have a sleep.

Carole recognized that this was very unusual behaviour from Jude. She also found it surprisingly difficult to persuade her neighbour that they should meet up later and have an early evening drink at the Crown & Anchor. Which again was most unlike Jude.

Her neighbour's mood seemed only to have improved a little when they met at six in Fethering's only pub. Later in the year that might have been the time when Carole would be walking her Labrador, Gulliver, but in January it was virtually dark by four o'clock.

There was no doubt, from the minute the two of them walked in, about what the Crown & Anchor's main topic of conversation was going to be that evening. The first words they heard from the shaggy-haired and bearded landlord Ted Crisp were, 'So, either of you two know anything about this stiff up at the library?'

'Why should we?' asked Carole.

'Well, you two are more in the range of literary types than me, aren't you? Ex-stand-up comics don't go in so much for the reading lark.'

'I know no more than what we've heard on the radio.'

'Ah. And does your intonation imply, by any chance, Carole, that, while *you* know no more, Jude perhaps *does* know more.'

'That wasn't what I meant to imply.' But Carole still looked at her neighbour expectantly, as if prompting some revelations.

The uncomfortable moment was interrupted by an accented voice saying, 'For heaven's sake, Ted. Are you forgetting what a landlord's job is? You are meant to ask your customers what they would like to drink.'

It was his Polish bar manager Zosia, of permanent blonde pigtails and normally permanent smile. Jude noticed, however, that that evening the girl's usual sparkle was absent. There was a sadness in her pale blue eyes. Jude, a creature of instant compassion, made a mental note.

Zosia had arrived in Fethering following the murder of her brother Tadeusz, and had become a fixture as bar manager of the Crown & Anchor. It was her efficiency, together with the culinary skills of the chef, Ed Pollack, which had transformed a shabby local into one of the go-to destinations on the South Coast. The hostelry had even been described by some online travel guides, in a term Ted Crisp loathed, as a 'gastropub'.

'I don't have to ask these two what they want to drink,' the landlord protested. 'It'll be a couple of large Sauvignon Blancs, won't it?'

'Well, if you know what they're going to drink, there's nothing to stop you pouring them out, is there?' Zosia tutted and sighed in a mock put-upon manner. 'I'll do it.' She reached for a bottle from the ice-filled tub on the counter.

The diversion had given Jude a moment to plan her response. Still feeling the shock of what had happened, she had no desire once again to go through the events of the night before. So, with a convincing giggle, she said, 'You shouldn't be asking us, Ted. We are, after all, in the Crown & Anchor, a much more efficient source of rumour and conspiracy theories than Facebook or Twitter. Compared to that, we know nothing. I'm sure you heard a few speculations about the death at lunchtime.'

'You're not wrong there. Yes, everyone had their own view of what had happened.'

'I'm surprised they even knew about it,' said Carole. 'We heard the news on *The World at One*.'

Jude flashed a quick smile of gratitude at her neighbour, who could easily have opened a whole can of worms by saying how the information had come into Woodside Cottage. But Jude knew she only had a brief reprieve before all Fethering would know about her connection to Burton St Clair. The news of the body's discovery had spread quickly, no doubt originating from Vix Winter, Di Thompson or someone else working at the library. It was only a matter of time before the knowledge of who had joined Burton in his BMW at the end of the evening was also revealed to the village.

For the time being, though, Jude knew she had to maintain her mask of insouciance. 'So, give us the headlines, Ted,' she said. 'Don't bother with the really wacky ones. Just tell us what Fethering's current theories are about the death?'

'Well, obviously, it's a murder . . .'

'Why "obviously"?' asked Carole.

'Because that's the way the good citizens of Fethering think. Basically, they've watched too much television. They've already named the case "The Body in the Library".'

'Oh, bad luck,' said Jude. 'I think they'll find that title's been used.'

'And, anyway,' Carole picked up, 'it's inappropriate. The body was not found *in* the library. It was found *outside* the library.'

Seeing that Ted was about to ask how her neighbour knew that, Jude came quickly in with, 'Doesn't have the same ring, does it? "The Body Outside the Library"? Anyway, who does Fethering reckon committed this ghastly crime?'

'Oh, they wheeled out the usual suspects. Russian intelligence agents, Romanian drug traffickers, Chinese triads from Brighton . . . And, of course, there were the regular moans about travellers and migrants – legal or illegal.'

Jude noticed a tiny reaction to Ted's last words from Zosia, who was standing behind him. She hoped that didn't indicate the bar manager had suffered any recent slights about her nationality. Though the nice middle-class people of Fethering liked to think of themselves as liberal and tolerant, the undercurrent of racial feeling in the village could all too easily come to the surface. Antisemitism sometimes reared its ugly head, and discussions of immigration could all too quickly lead to a kind of kneejerk xenophobia . . . though of course in Fethering all such thoughts were expressed in the best possible taste.

'So,' asked Carole, 'no theories about the death that sounded vaguely plausible?'

'Ah now, I didn't say that. There were a couple of very interesting theories put forward, of course unimpeded by any knowledge of the facts . . .'

'. . . as is customary in the speculations of Fethering . . .'

'Exactly, Carole, yes. Well, a theory that was put forward quite convincingly by one of the lunchtime regulars – don't think you know him, tends to spend his evenings in the Yacht Club. Anyway, he said that the victim, whoever he was, was a writer—'

'That's true.'

'And he'd just had a big success with some book . . .'

'*Stray Leaves in Autumn.*'

'Title doesn't mean anything to me. I'm not much of a reader. Anyway, this Hercule Poirot of the Yacht Club, he reckoned that the murder must've been done out of jealousy by a less successful author. He says that kind of thing's always happening in literary circles.'

'And he doesn't base this on any inside knowledge?' asked Carole.

'No inside knowledge, no outside knowledge, no knowledge of any kind – like I said, as usual in Fethering.'

'Yes.'

'You mentioned "a couple of theories",' said Jude. 'What was the other one?'

'Right. This was some American woman sounding off.'

'Did you know her, Ted?'

'Never seen her before in my life. Anyway, she said that this kind of murder is almost always domestic, and it always starts with the husband having an affair. Then she said there are three possible scenarios that can happen, and she gave each of them, like titles. Now what was it . . .?' His eyes beneath their shaggy brows screwed up with the effort of recollection. 'Yes, "HKW" . . . "WKM" . . . Those were the first two.'

'And what in heaven's name do they mean?' asked Carole.

'"HKW" means "Husband Kills Wife", and "WKM" means "Wife Kills Mistress".'

'Well, neither of those works in this case,' she observed tartly, 'because it's the husband who got killed.'

'Yes, I know that. Now, what were the other categories she had . . .?'

'You seem to remember her words very clearly,' said Jude, 'if this was just a casual conversation.'

'I do remember them well, because she talked like she was a teacher. Whole bar went quiet when she started, everyone was listening to her.'

'Was she very tall?' asked Jude. 'And blonde?'

'Yes, she was. Why, do you know her?'

'No. It's just there was someone at the library talk yesterday who fitted that description. She said she taught mystery fiction.'

'Do people actually *teach* that?' asked a bemused Ted.

'You bet. Particularly in the States.'

'Oh.'

'Anyway,' said Carole, wanting to move the conversation on, 'what was this woman's view of the current case?'

Again, the landlord screwed up his eyes. 'Right, she said in this case we were up against either "WKH" or "MKL" . . .'

'"Wife Kills Husband" or "Mistress Kills Lover",' Carole translated unnecessarily.

'Yes. Or—' Ted Crisp concluded with some triumph – '"WAMKH".'

'"Wife And Mistress Kill Husband",' said Jude drily.

'You're spot on! So, this American bossy-boots reckoned all you got to do is to . . . "churchy"? "Churchy" something . . .? She said it was French.'

'*Cherchez la femme*?' Carole suggested.

'That's it – right. She said all you got to do is find out who in Fethering this writer chap had ever had an affair with – and she'll be your murderer!'

Jude didn't like the look her neighbour was giving her. She knew, however much she insisted she was telling the truth, Carole would still believe that there had once been something between Jude and Burton.

And if Carole thought that, it would only be a matter of time before the rest of Fethering thought the same.

EIGHT

The wine and the company in the Crown & Anchor had cheered Jude up, but when she said goodnight to Carole at the gate of Woodside Cottage, she felt the darkness closing in again. The reality of Burton's death and the unpleasant recollection of her police interview in the morning dominated her mind.

It wasn't yet eight o'clock and she hadn't had anything to eat since Carole's cottage cheese salad, so she knew she ought to be assembling some kind of supper. But the urge wasn't there. She didn't feel hungry.

Jude opened the laptop to check her emails. There was one from Megan. It read simply: 'Yes, we should be in touch.' No 'Love'. No 'Good Wishes'. No home address. Just a mobile number.

Jude consulted the large-faced watch fixed to her wrist by a broad ribbon. It was a perfectly reasonable hour to ring someone. She dialled the number.

'Hello?' The voice was breathless and slightly actressy. But also guarded, cautious, as if expecting a call it didn't want to take. Very familiar, though. Though they had been such close friends, Jude remembered the voice's tautness, its owner's inability ever quite to relax, her habit of watchfulness, always anticipating some kind of slight.

'Megan, it's Jude.'

'Ah. I thought you'd probably be in touch quite soon.' Megan made it sound as though Jude's quick response was in some way shameful.

'I just wanted to say I heard about Burton . . . Al.'

'Well, of course you did. You were there when it happened.'

'You know that because the police have talked to you?'

'I was spending a long weekend with a friend in Scarborough.' So Detective Sergeant Knight's information had been correct.

'There was no mobile signal at her place. I only found out they'd been trying to contact me when I got on the train. I rang them as soon as I could. They checked out my alibi with my friend. It was when I was talking to Detective Inspector Rollins that I found out about you being there.'

'Let's be clear, Megan, I was at Fethering Library for his talk in the evening. I wasn't actually there when he died.'

'No, of course not.'

Again, there was an edge of scepticism in the voice. Jude was the last person in the world to get paranoid, but events of the last twenty-four hours had unsettled her deeply.

'I think we ought to meet, Megan.'

'As I said in my email, yes, I think we should.'

'Where do you live now?'

'Still in Morden.'

'Oh.'

'The same house. I got it as part of the divorce settlement.'

Jude didn't have a car. Morden was the southernmost stop of the Northern Line. Trains from Fethering terminated at Victoria. 'Probably make sense if we were to meet in London . . . what, for lunch maybe?' she suggested.

'I don't go to London,' said Megan.

'What?' Jude reminded herself that she was talking to Megan Georgeson, who at the height of her television fame was photographed at every first night and queened it into the small hours at the Groucho Club and Soho House. Her not going to London was inconceivable. 'What do you mean?'

'I don't go to London,' Megan repeated with no further explanation.

'Well, do you want me to come to the house?'

'No, I don't like people coming to the house. That's an invasion of my privacy.'

Jude tried to keep the exasperation out of her voice as she asked, 'Is there anywhere you would like to meet?'

'There's a restaurant in Morden called Ancient Persia. I go there quite often. The owners know me.'

'So, shall we meet there?'

'Very well.' Megan made it sound as though she was making a big concession.

'When? I think it should be as soon as possible.'

'I agree.'

'Tomorrow?'

There was a moment of hesitation from the other end of the line. 'Yes, all right.'

'Fine.'

'One o'clock. Ancient Persia.'

Jude had a couple of healing sessions set up for the Thursday, but she rang the clients and rescheduled them. This was unusual. In her professional life, her loyalty to her clients was paramount. She knew how dependent they were on their regular therapy. That she took such action was a measure of how important she considered her meeting with Megan Sinclair to be.

There was probably an easier way to get from Fethering to Morden by public transport, but Jude didn't investigate it. Carole, she knew would have done, but Jude was content to get the train from Fethering Station to Victoria, get to the south-bound Northern Line and stay on the tube as far as it went.

She had taken a book with her, a treatise a friend had written about the relationship between the NHS and complementary medicine, but her gaze kept sliding off the page. She was tired; the last night had been a troubled one, though that wasn't the only reason for her poor concentration. Thoughts whirled around her head in unaccustomed agitation. And for some reason, she felt worried about the forthcoming encounter with Megan. Her old friend's manner on the phone had set up a barrier between them. And, though Jude was not a person to let grievances fester, she did not think their meeting was going to be an easy one.

Getting off at the underground station was familiar from the many times she'd made the journey to visit the newly married Sinclairs, but when she emerged she found herself in a slightly different Morden from the one of twenty years before. Then it had been a depressed, dreary outer suburb. But, as house prices in London rocketed, even well-heeled commuters found them-selves having to move further away from the centre to find an affordable family house. Places like Morden were suddenly in danger of becoming trendy. The change hadn't happened yet; it was a work in progress. Morden remained a depressed, dreary outer suburb, but one perhaps on the verge of gentrification.

Jude noticed a few more coffee shops and restaurants than there had been before. Some of them even had seats and tables outside, supporting England's doomed attempt to recreate what people liked to call 'café society' (which will never quite work until there's a change in the country's weather). In January, the only people sitting outside were desperate cigarette-puffers driven there by the smoking ban.

The Ancient Persia was a sign of the change to come. It didn't look ancient at all. Nor particularly Persian. But it did look very new. Apart from a couple of tall, non-functioning hookahs by way of set dressing, everything else was scrubbed wood, stainless steel and glass. It was one of the new wave of exotically ethnic restaurants that were invading all parts of London. Though giving the impression of individuality, most of them were parts of chains. Equally 'individual' Ancient Persias could be found in Shoreditch, Crouch End and Stoke Newington. The fact that one had opened in Morden was a very encouraging sign for the area. Waitrose might come next.

The first thing that struck Jude about Megan, already sitting at the table, was her size. It was at least twenty years since they had last met and Jude knew that the menopause could be cruel. She herself had put on the pounds, but nothing to compare with the scale on which Megan had. She had given up 'waiflike' for 'tubby'. Her once 'surprisingly' blue eyes had sunk into rolls of flesh. No one now would speak of her 'fragile beauty' without irony. Nor, to be uncharitably accurate, would anyone speak of any kind of beauty. Megan Georgeson, having flitted for some years through the steamy dreams of so many male television viewers, in her fifties had transformed into a dumpy woman to whom no one would have given a second glance.

She didn't rise to meet Jude. She stayed in her seat with a half-empty glass of wine in front of her. 'Long time no see,' she drawled, in what now sounded like a parody of her theatrical voice.

Jude followed her instinct and did what she would have

done with any of her friends, arms round neck and a kiss. The gesture wasn't made easier by the recipient's seated immobility.

As Jude took her seat opposite, Megan said, 'Well, there's a lot more of you than when we last met.'

It wasn't in Jude's nature to snap back with a line about pots and kettles. Instead, she chuckled. 'Which of us can resist the march of the years, eh?'

Megan laughed cynically and downed her remaining wine. 'Must get some more of this. Do you drink red?'

'Well, I usually—'

But her friend wasn't listening. She waved to a purple-jacketed waiter who was taking the order from an adjacent table. 'Cyrus,' she called, and held her two hands apart at the height of a bottle. Cyrus nodded to acknowledge the order. Clearly Megan was a regular at the Ancient Persia. Also, it seemed, a regular drinker.

'Still on the red wine, I see,' Jude observed. 'Al always liked his red wine, didn't he?'

'Red wine, beer, whisky. He liked everything alcoholic. Hardly ever left the house without his little hipflask of Scotch – but you remember that, don't you, Jude?'

'I'm not sure I—'

'Of course you do.' Megan reached for her glass and was disappointed to be reminded it was empty.

Jude was beginning to feel their conversation had got off on the wrong foot. So, perhaps belatedly, she said, 'I suppose I should be offering you condolences about Al's death.'

'Why? He's nothing to do with me. He hasn't been anything to do with me for fifteen years.'

'Maybe not, but—'

'Anyway, why should I care what's happened to the bastard? He screwed up my life pretty thoroughly. Five wasted years of marriage, and then I discovered the slime-ball was screwing everything in sight. I had a complete breakdown after the divorce – did you know that?'

'No. I'm sorry.'

'Well, you wouldn't know, would you? Never heard from you after the marriage ended, did I?'

'I tried ringing a good few times, left messages, but you never got back to me.'

'Really? Didn't I? How remiss of me.' Megan's tone implied that no such messages had ever been sent.

'I can assure you I—'

Jude was interrupted by the arrival at their table of the waiter, Cyrus. He unscrewed the wine bottle and filled their two glasses. Then he poised his pen over his notepad. 'Are you ready to order?'

'I'll have the usual,' said Megan.

'Of course.' He wrote it down '*Fesenjan.*'

'What's that?' asked Jude.

'It is a very traditional Persian dish,' the waiter replied. 'Chicken with ground walnuts and pomegranate – very good.'

'I'll have the same.' She hadn't had an opportunity to look at the menu, but wanted to get back to challenging Megan's accusations of disloyalty. As Cyrus moved away, she picked up, 'I can assure you I did everything to try and contact you, but got no response.'

'Oh well, water under the bridge.' But Megan didn't say it in a forgiving way. 'So, the marriage took five years out of my life, the breakdown took two – more than that, actually. I'm still not shot of the symptoms. And when I'm finally in a state to pick up my career, I ring my agent and – surprise, surprise – there haven't been any recent enquiries for my services. The news of my illness had somehow got out, and who wants to employ an actor who's got mental problems? Making television is such an expensive process, producers can't risk casting someone who might crack up at any moment. So bye-bye, career.

'And of course that bastard Al was always stringing me along about having children. He knew I wanted to, but he kept putting it off.'

Jude's own view was that Al Sinclair had never wanted children. He was one of those men whose ego was so huge he didn't want his women's adoration of him to be diluted by any other demands. But she kept that opinion to herself, saying, 'To be fair, your television career was doing so well at that time, you wouldn't have wanted to interrupt—'

'I would have dropped it all in a moment to have a baby!'

Megan was now in full tragic heroine mode. Jude didn't believe her, but understood how she had refashioned her past into something she now thought was the truth.

'Well, I'm sorry, but—'

'You never had children, did you, Jude?' Megan looked at her beadily.

'No.'

'And doesn't it make you feel dreadful?'

'No,' Jude replied, evenly and honestly. 'The right time and the right man never coincided.'

'Al was the right man for me, and I'm sure if we'd had a baby we could have saved the marriage.'

Jude disagreed completely. Having Megan tied to the house by a baby would have just given someone like Al Sinclair further scope for his infidelities. But there was no point in saying anything. Nothing would shift Megan from the version of the past that she had forged.

'Well, who knows?' said Jude, resorting to a safe platitude.

'*I* know,' Megan responded. 'The point about being married to a bastard like Al is that . . .'

Fortunately, the diatribe was stopped by the arrival of Cyrus with their *fesenjan*. The dark brown stew, served on a bed of rice and garnished with pomegranate seeds, smelt wonderful, rich and warming, perfect for an icy January day.

Cyrus refilled their wine glasses. Megan's was empty; Jude's only needed topping up. And that wasn't because of her preference for white wine. She was finding the Shiraz they were drinking quite acceptable. It was just that Megan was drinking faster than she was.

The *fesenjan* was as delicious as it smelt: rich, creamy and probably devastating to the waistline. For a moment, there was a silence as the two women started eating.

Then Megan said, 'Pity Al isn't with us today.'

'No, it's very sad that—'

'I didn't mean that.'

'Oh?'

Megan's next words were accompanied by a vicious grin. 'I mean, that this would kill him.' She gestured to their *fesenjan*.

'What do you mean?'

'Oh, come on, Jude, don't pretend you've forgotten.'

'Forgotten what?'

'That Al was allergic to walnuts. For God's sake, he was always going on about it. Turned it into a drama, like everything else in his life. Never went anywhere without his EpiPen. Kept going on about "spending his life on the edge of death". Seemed to think it turned him into a tragic doomed artist, like bloody Keats. Oh, Jude, of course you knew about it.'

'I'm sorry, I didn't.'

'Oh well, if that's the way you want to play it . . .' She took another big swallow of wine. Once again, her glass was emptying considerably faster than Jude's.

'Megan, you seem to be under the misapprehension that I knew a lot more about Al than I did.'

'What, you stopped listening to him after a while, did you? I know what you mean. I did the same. He did go on a bit, didn't he? But I thought you'd have taken in the information about his precious allergy, given how much time you spent together.'

'We didn't spend any time together. I don't think Al and I ever spent more than ten minutes together without you present.'

Megan let out a little cynical laugh. 'OK, if that's your story, stick with it, by all means.'

'It's not a story.' Jude seemed to have been closer to anger in the last thirty-six hours than she had for a very long time. 'It's the truth.'

'Then why were you suddenly so keen to get in touch with me? And don't tell me it had anything to do with Al's Seth Marston books.'

'That was the original reason.'

'But then, when Al's death became public, you had other reasons to contact me.'

'The main one being that the police contacted me.'

'And that got you worried?'

'I wouldn't say that.'

'No? Detective Inspector Rollins, was it?'

'Yes.'

'I spent a long time talking to her yesterday.'

'Right.'

Megan smiled complacently, not about to divulge what she and the Inspector had talked about. 'And Rollins got you worried, did she?'

'Not particularly.'

'Oh, come on, Jude. You're not going to persuade me that you were so keen to see me just to offer condolences?'

'I'm not saying that. Offering condolences was obviously part of—'

'Anyway,' Megan interrupted, 'shouldn't it be me offering condolences to you? You loved Al a lot more than I ever did.'

'What?'

'As soon as he was on the scene, you seemed to be round all the time.'

'We saw no more of each other than we did when you were single.'

'Rubbish!'

'You were my friend. When Al came along, I was just pleased you'd found someone, that's all.'

'If that's all, why did you see so much of us then?' asked Megan aggressively. 'It wasn't me you wanted to see once Al was around.'

'Don't be ridiculous.'

'Ridiculous? As I mentioned, I haven't noticed much sign of you being in touch with me since the divorce. Whereas I'm sure you and Al have been permanently "in touch".'

'Megan, that is absolute nonsense. Till he contacted me about his talk in Fethering Library, I'd hardly heard from him since the divorce.'

'You and I haven't been in touch since then either,' said Megan, rather wistfully.

'I know we haven't, and I regret that much more. You were the one I wanted to keep in touch with.'

For a moment, there was a softness in Megan's eyes, a flicker of the friendship that had once existed between them. But it vanished very quickly, and she was back on the attack. 'In spite of that, it was Burton who knew you lived in Fethering, wasn't it? I didn't know that.'

'I assume he heard through a mutual friend. I certainly didn't tell him.'

'No?' Megan gave a weary sigh, topped up her wine glass and took a long swallow. 'You can stop pretending, Jude. I know that your affair with Al started soon after our wedding. And it was your affair with Al that broke up a perfectly good marriage.'

'That is just not true!' In her shock, Jude spoke louder than she'd intended. A few of the other customers looked with characteristically English embarrassment towards their table.

'Oh, I know what's true,' Megan assured her. And Jude realized how firmly the details of her recreated past had taken root in the woman's mind.

'And did you tell Detective Inspector Rollins about what you've just accused me of?'

'Of course.' Megan smiled complacently. 'When you're questioned by the police, you have to tell the truth, Jude. Surely you know that?'

NINE

On the train back from Victoria, Jude had a call on her mobile from Detective Inspector Rollins. She didn't answer it. Partly this was because she didn't want to share such potentially sensitive subject matter with a carriage-full of commuters. But also she wanted a bit of time to digest her encounter with Megan Sinclair.

The main feeling it had left her with was not resentment that her actions had been so traduced, but sadness. Before her marriage, Megan and she had been very close, but now that relationship was irreparably damaged. Her gloomy prognostications of the morning had proved justified. Jude found herself mourning the loss of a friend.

She also found herself chilled to the bone. In another of a series of lapses by Southern Rail, on that day, one of the coldest of the year, the heating in the carriages wasn't working.

It was late afternoon when she arrived back at Woodside Cottage. Immediately she put on leggings, two jumpers, the central heating and an electric fire. For good measure, she lit the open fire in her sitting room.

She had intended to ring Rollins the moment she got in, but was waylaid by a message on her answering machine.

'Hello, it's Oliver Parsons. We met at the library the other evening. I hope you don't mind my calling. I got your number from the phonebook. I just thought that, further to our conversation at the library . . . well, things have turned out rather surprisingly, haven't they? Bit of a shock, what happened to our speaker, wouldn't you say? Anyway, I just thought . . . if you'd like to talk about it further, give me a call.' He provided his mobile number. 'Look forward to hearing from you . . . maybe?'

His voice, she remembered, was urbane, slightly teasing. And there was more than a hint of flirtatiousness in his final 'maybe?' Jude also wondered about the truth of his assertion that he'd found her name in the phonebook. It was certainly there, but under one of her married surnames, 'Nicholls'. Few people knew that. She reckoned Oliver Parsons would have had to do a bit of research to track it down. Which was interesting . . . possibly even flattering.

She had no hesitation in deferring contact with Detective Inspector Rollins and calling Oliver Parsons instead. The more information she could get about what had happened on the Tuesday night, the better equipped she would feel to face another interrogation from the police.

'Hello, Jude. How very nice to hear from you.' Again, the warmth and gratifying enthusiasm in his voice.

'I was just ringing to say: thanks for your message.'

'And does this mean you would like to talk further about Tuesday night?'

'It does.'

'Excellent. As I believe I mentioned at the library, I have – had – an interest in crime fiction. But crime fact is so much more exciting.'

'What makes you think there's actually a crime involved?

Her question seemed to throw him for a moment, then he replied smoothly, 'One has only to listen to the views of anyone in Fethering. They're all certain that Burton St Clair was murdered. And from all accounts, the police are crawling all over the village. Would they do that in the case of a natural death?'

Jude recognized that it was a moment for her to be discreet. 'Who knows? I'm not very familiar with the workings of the constabulary.'

'Nor me. Well, that is to say, I am only familiar with the workings of the constabulary in Golden Age crime fiction, when all it involved was being in a state of perpetual bafflement and waiting around for a polymathic amateur sleuth to come and solve the case.'

'But where do you find a polymathic amateur sleuth in Fethering?'

'Where indeed? Anyway, you would be happy to meet up and talk about the "case"?'

'Yes.'

'Maybe meet for a drink sometime?'

'That would suit me. The Crown & Anchor?'

'Ooh, I think not. Anything that happens in the Crown & Anchor is shared within seconds by *le tout* Fethering. I would advocate somewhere a little further off the radar.'

'Fine. You tell me where.'

'I could give you a lift there . . . since you don't have a car.'

'How do you know I don't have a car?'

'If you had a car, why would you be accepting Burton St Clair's offer to drive you home on Tuesday?'

'Fair enough. When do you want to meet?'

'When you like, Jude. The end at which I am is permanently loose these days.'

'I could do this evening.'

'How serendipitous. So could I. Tell me when and I'll be outside Woodside Cottage at the appointed hour.'

'Six?'

'Perfect.'

Jude had an hour to bathe and change clothes. Megan and Morden needed cleansing from her body. And the bones within that body needed the chill of Southern Rail thawed out of them.

She didn't dress with any particular thoughtfulness for her

meeting with Oliver Parsons. Or at least, that's what she told herself.

Somehow, within the hour she'd had before he was scheduled to arrive, she didn't find time to get back to Detective Inspector Rollins.

Oliver Parsons appeared at the appointed hour in a black Range Rover which looked huge in the street outside Woodside Cottage. He escorted Jude rather gallantly from her front door to the passenger side. Not wishing to repeat her sartorial insouciance of the Tuesday, she wore a thick woollen coat. And she needed it. In her brief journey to the car the air stung her cheeks. Inside, of course, all was toasty warmth.

'Am I allowed to know where we're going?' she asked once they were under way.

'The Hare & Hounds at Weldisham. Do you know it?'

'Oh yes.' The pub had featured prominently in one of Carole and Jude's earlier investigations, which had been started by the discovery of some human bones in a barn near the village.

But when she and Oliver entered the Hare & Hounds that cold January evening, Jude saw that it had had yet another makeover. When she first saw it, the place had been all old tennis rackets, 1930s novel and pike in glass cases, in the style of a country house weekend party. On a more recent visit she had found the interior and the staff liveried in pale grey. Now everything was consciously mismatched: tables in a variety of sizes whose scrubbed surfaces were a colour chart of different wood tones, and a gallimaufry of different wooden chairs.

But with each incarnation of the Hare & Hounds, one trend was constant. The bar got smaller and the restaurant got bigger. Less and less were country pubs venues where the locals might slip in for a pint. Managements knew that their profit lay in the food.

Oliver Parsons, who was clearly used to squiring women around, found them seats at a table near the open fire. Jude, grateful for its heat and still remembering Southern Rail, kept her coat on while he went to get their drinks. He returned with a large New Zealand Sauvignon Blanc and a pint of Sussex Gold.

Toasts completed, he said, 'On the phone I mentioned rumours of a strong police presence in Fethering. Have you seen any sign of them?'

'Oh yes. They've been in touch with me.'

He looked puzzled. 'Why?'

'Last person to be seen with the deceased. Come on, Oliver, surely your reading of Golden Age crime fiction has taught you that someone in that position is bound to be the police's first suspect . . . at least until eliminated from their enquiries.'

'And have you been "eliminated from their enquiries"?'

Jude wished she could have given a more positive reply than 'I have to hope so.'

'Hm. So what were the circumstances of you being the last person to see him alive?'

'Well, you heard him offering me a lift home?'

'Yes.'

'But you didn't hear whether or not I accepted the lift?'

'I didn't.'

'Well, I knew it was out of his way, so I walked home.' While the facts were accurate, Jude knew that she was lying by omission.

'So how come you were the last person to see him alive?'

'As soon as they'd locked up, the two librarians went off in Di's car. I was still there, saying goodbye to Burton. Then I walked home.'

'In the pouring rain?'

'Yes.'

He seemed about to follow on from this, but fortunately he didn't. Instead, he changed tack and asked, 'Presumably, when the police spoke to you, they didn't mention the word "murder"?'

'Oh no, they're far too canny for that. "Just making routine enquiries."' Again, she would have preferred to be more certain that they were just routine enquiries. 'They haven't talked to you yet, have they, Oliver?'

He looked a little shaken by the suggestion. 'No, why should they?'

'Well, presumably, if they do continue to believe that there's foul play involved, they will be contacting everyone who was present at Burton's final appearance in Fethering Library.'

'Yes, I suppose they might.' He sounded intrigued by the idea. Then, almost hopefully, he asked, 'You say "if they continue to believe that there's foul play involved". That doesn't mean . . .?'

'No, sorry to disappoint you, Oliver, but they didn't use the expression "foul play" any more than they used the word "murder".'

'Ah. I was afraid you'd say that.'

There was a companionable silence. Jude undid the buttons of her coat as the fire's warmth spread through her body. She was enjoying the Sauvignon Blanc much more than she had enjoyed what little she'd got of the Shiraz at lunchtime. The company was more relaxed.

'If this were a Golden Age murder mystery . . .' Oliver began slowly, 'and we were two amateur sleuths . . .'

'*Polymathic* amateur sleuths?'

'Let's not go that far. Just amateur. Anyway, if we were, we would now be going through everything we'd seen happen last Tuesday night at Fethering Library and extracting clues. We would be comparing notes on everyone's suspicious behaviour.'

'Including our own?'

'Let's exclude ourselves for the moment, Jude.'

'And then we can have a startling revelation in the penultimate chapter that one of us was actually the murderer?'

He chuckled. 'Yes, all right, if you like. But who was behaving suspiciously on Tuesday?'

'Well, assuming that Burton St Clair was murdered . . . and that is a very big assumption . . . But if he was, then the person who behaved most aggressively towards him, who actually threatened him, was your friend from the Writers' Group.'

'Hardly my *friend*. But you mean Steve Chasen?'

'Yes. I'd forgotten his name. But the one whose genius as a writer of science fiction had yet to be recognized by an insensitive and misguided world.'

'That's Steve. He's one of those people who from time to time has to be hospitalized, so that he can have more chips put on his shoulders.'

Jude chuckled. 'Not a million miles from Al – Burton St Clair – in that respect. But do you know if there was any history between them?'

'You mean: did Steve actually know Burton?' Oliver shrugged.
'If he did, he never mentioned the fact in my hearing.'

'Then why would he be so aggressive towards him?'

'You don't know Steve. He's aggressive towards everyone,
but particularly people who are successful in the writing game.
A conspiracy theorist, he regards every published author to be
part of the conspiracy against him. They only had their books
published in order to prevent him having his published.'

'I see. So his ranting against Burton wasn't anything
personal?'

'No, he's got form. He's barracked other visiting writers in
Fethering Library. In fact, thinking about it, I'm surprised
Di Thompson let him in on Tuesday.'

'And the drinking?'

'Oh, he's got form there too. A bit of a sad case, really, but
one of those sad cases who behaves so obnoxiously it's hard
to feel any sympathy for them. I dare say you've come across
some of those in your work as a healer . . .?'

Jude nodded, but made no further comment. She was very
strict about client confidentiality. 'I was just thinking, Oliver,
if we go along with the prevalent Fethering view that Burton
St Clair was murdered . . .'

'Yes?'

'. . . have we any idea what killed him?'

'No.' His forehead wrinkled in frustration. 'Police are very
reluctant these days to share their information with amateur
sleuths. Oh, if only we were back in the Golden Age – Lord
Peter Wimsey is lacking a vital forensic detail and Inspector
Parker, tugging his metaphorical forelock, immediately shares
with him the findings of the police post-mortem. Don't get that
kind of co-operation now. Police no longer know their place.
They are even . . .' he chuckled as he framed the witticism
'. . . getting ideas above their *station*.'

Jude winced. 'Ooh, that's dreadful.'

He didn't argue. 'So, my dear, not having any helpful police
information to rely on, we must resort to conjecture. Was Burton
St Clair perhaps shot, stabbed or strangled in his car?'

She shrugged. 'All possible, I suppose. But, following our
Golden Age theme, let's concentrate on a "Murder in the Library".

And ask ourselves: was there any way whereby his life could have been cruelly curtailed before he left the premises?'

'What, and then dragged out to his car? But you said you saw the library doors locked by Di Thompson.'

'Yes, I was thinking of other methods, though. Poison?'

'Ah.' Oliver Parsons looked at her nearly empty glass. 'Time for refills. What's your poison?'

Jude winced at the pleasantry, before saying, 'It's my turn.'

'Nonsense. This whole meeting was my idea, so it's my treat.'

Jude didn't buy the argument, but made no objection. She slipped her coat off her shoulders. For the first time since meeting Megan, she felt warm.

Oliver returned with the order as before. 'Poison as a murder method . . .?' he said, once they were settled with their drinks. 'Very much in the Golden Age tradition, of course. How could Burton St Clair have been poisoned in the library?'

'I didn't see him eat anything, so it must have been in his drink.'

'The conjectural poison must have been in his drink?' Oliver was slightly sending her up with his scepticism.

'Exactly. Which means it was either in the water he drank during his talk or the wine he drank after it.'

'The wine came from bottles everyone else was having their glasses filled from. There hasn't been news of a massive death toll of Fethering library-goers, has there?'

'Not that I've heard of, no.' Jude didn't think it was the moment to mention Burton's walnut allergy. She and Oliver Parsons were really just playing games. She didn't want too much reality to intrude into their speculation.

Increasingly she was beginning to think that Oliver's interest in Burton St Clair's death was just an excuse to get to know her better. And, increasingly, the more time she spent with him, she found herself warming to the prospect.

'So I think, Jude, we should probably concentrate on the water he drank during his talk. As I recall, it came from a half-litre plastic bottle. I didn't notice the brand. Did you?'

'No.'

'But if there were poison put into that bottle, we have to ask ourselves who would have had the opportunity to put it there?'

'I think there can only be two suspects. The two librarians. Di Thompson and Vix Winter.'

'Why do you say that?'

'Well, think about it. Presumably they were the only ones there when Burton arrived. They'd have set up the room, moved the chairs and so on. They would also have put up the screens from his publishers, and made everything else ready for his talk, setting up his table and chair . . . and his water bottle and glass.'

'I suppose you're right. So perhaps we should be investigating Di Thompson and Vix Winter.'

'Perhaps we should.' Though why? Jude wondered. She herself had a personal interest in the case; the attitude of the police made her want to remove her name firmly from their list of suspects. But why was Oliver Parsons so interested? She asked him.

'Oh, my interest arises, like so many things in my life, from sheer idleness. Or do I mean boredom? As I said, for a while I got fascinated by reading about amateur sleuths. Now I'm fascinated, at least for the time being, by the idea of being one. It's just a game, nothing more than that.'

'You enjoy playing games?'

'Oh yes.'

'Well then, let's move to the next stage of the game . . .'

'Very well.'

'. . . and imagine what would happen if the poison was not in the water that Burton drank, but in the wine . . .?'

'I'm happy to run with that.'

'I was thinking back to last Tuesday, and when Burton actually got his glass of wine. There was some confusion, as I recall.'

'That's right.' Oliver snapped his fingers unconsciously as he tried to visualize the scene. 'They'd run out of red, and the junior went into the staff room to get another bottle. And I think Di went in too.'

'She did. Yes, she seemed quite keen to get away from Burton, I remember.'

'And why would that be?'

'If past form's anything to go by, Oliver, it would be because he'd just made a pass at her.'

'Ah. Right.'

The scene was now coming back very vividly to Jude. 'Then suddenly both librarians were bustling Steve Chasen out of the staff room. And you told him he'd had too much to drink and helped him on his way out of the main doors. And Vix said something about a wine bottle having been knocked over . . .'

'And Di said Steve had been responsible . . .'

'And Vix said she'd clear it up. So, if we are going down our poison in the wine scenario . . .' Jude began to sum up, 'Steve Chasen went into the staff room . . .'

'Ostensibly to get himself a glass of wine, but in fact to put poison in the bottle from which Burton's glass would be poured; and then, once it had been poured, he knocked over the bottle, to ensure that no one else got poisoned . . .'

'And Vix Winter cleaned up the mess, which effectively removed any evidence of the crime that had been committed . . .'

Glowing with triumph, Jude's eyes engaged with Oliver's. His looked equally triumphant.

'I think the next thing we have to do,' he said, 'is to talk to Steve Chasen.'

Jude didn't object to his use of the word 'we'. In fact, she rather liked it.

She had enjoyed her evening. It had been fun playing amateur sleuths with Oliver Parsons. And as he dropped her outside Woodside Cottage she looked up at High Tor with a slight feeling of guilt. After all, it was Carole with whom she usually played amateur sleuths.

TEN

Jude's first client wasn't booked till two p.m., so she didn't hurry to get up in the morning. The world beneath her duvet was a comfortingly warm one. And her evening with Oliver Parsons had done much to restore the spirits brought down by her encounter with Megan Sinclair.

Though she had not realized until getting home, her mobile had stayed on her bedroom table while she was at the Hare & Hounds. There was another message on it from Detective Inspector Rollins. And one on the landline. Jude didn't feel inclined to answer them in a hurry.

Around eight-thirty in the morning she went down to the kitchen for long enough to make herself a cup of coffee and then crawled back to bed with it. She didn't read or put on the radio, she just enjoyed the snugness.

This feeling was increased when, on the dot of nine, she had a call from Oliver. He said how much he'd enjoyed their evening. 'And, what's more, I have made a positive move following it.'

'What do you mean?'

'Left a message with Steve Chasen. Said I'd like to meet.'

'Do you think he'll get back to you?'

'I'm certain he will. I said I had some other ideas of publishers to whom he could offer his science-fiction novel.'

'You're a crafty bastard.'

'Thank you. I take that as the compliment I'm sure it was meant to be. I'll let you know when I hear back from him. You must come along too when we meet up.'

'And how will you explain my presence?'

'I'll say you're a literary agent.'

She must have gone back to sleep again, because when she was wakened by the ringing of the doorbell, her watch told her it was nearly ten.

She tugged on a woollen dressing gown and went downstairs. When she opened the front door, she found herself confronted by Rollins and Knight.

'Good morning, Mrs Nicholls,' said the Detective Inspector.

'I told you "Jude" was—'

'I left a series of messages, to which you didn't reply.'

I know. I—'

'Didn't it occur to you that not getting back to me might make it look as though you had something to hide?'

And didn't it occur to you that I might have other demands on my time? Jude was shocked by how near she had been to saying the words out loud. The last thing she needed to do at that moment was to antagonize the police any more.

'May we come in? We need to talk to you.'

'Yes, of course.' Jude moved back into the hall. 'Do you mind if I just go up and put some clothes on?'

'Very well,' said Detective Inspector Rollins. 'This may take some time.'

'Do sit down. I'll make you some tea or coffee when I've—'

'We don't need any, thank you,' said Rollins.

'No, we don't,' confirmed Knight, not willing to be left out.

It was not in Jude's nature to feel guilty. In her personal and professional relationships, she was scrupulous about her honesty towards other people. And, unlike some people, she never felt the necessity to feel responsible for events over which she had no control.

But, as she quickly dressed in her customary layers of floaty garments up in her bedroom, she could not deny that she felt uneasy. She didn't need convincing of her own innocence, but she feared that bringing Detective Inspector Rollins round to the same view might be an uphill struggle.

So it proved. Having once again refused the offer of a drink, Rollins sat strictly upright, iPhone on lap, resisting the cushioned comfort of one of Jude's quilt-shrouded sofas, and said, 'Further evidence that has emerged means we are now seriously considering the possibility that Burton St Clair was murdered.'

Jude contemplated some remark about the people of Fethering being way ahead of the Detective Inspector in that conclusion, but decided it wasn't the moment. Instead, she stayed silent and listened as Rollins went on, 'The cause of his death seems to have been anaphylactic shock. Do I need to explain to you what that is?'

'No, I know. It's a violent allergic reaction.'

'And do you know what Burton St Clair was allergic to?'

'Walnuts.' There was no point in lying.

Rollins and Knight exchanged looks, as though something they had discussed earlier had been confirmed. 'So you knew about his walnut allergy?'

'Well, I've known since lunchtime yesterday.'

'When you met Megan Sinclair?' the Detective Sergeant contributed.

'Yes.

'You are saying,' asked Rollins, 'that until yesterday you did not know about Burton St Clair's walnut allergy?'

'That is exactly what I am saying.'

The Detective Inspector touched her iPhone to wake up the screen and looked down at it. 'That is not what Megan Sinclair says.'

'So, what does Megan Sinclair say?'

'She says that you've known about it for a long time. Twenty years? She says Burton told you about it very soon after you first met.'

'I have no recollection of that.'

'Don't you?' Rollins's tone made Jude realize how unconvincing her assertion sounded.

'Megan Sinclair recalled very distinctly the occasion when he told you about it.'

'It's not something I remember.'

'Are you saying you've forgotten being told that piece of information?'

'No, I am saying that, so far as I can recall, I was never given that piece of information.'

'"As far as I can recall",' came the sceptical echo. 'So, you're saying you might have been given that information and you might have forgotten about it?'

Jude's cool was being severely tested, but she was determined not to lose it. 'I am saying that when Megan mentioned the allergy yesterday, it was news to me. I hadn't heard about it before.'

'I see.' It was amazing how much reproach Rollins could get into two words.

Detective Sergeant Knight took up the baton of interrogation. 'Knowing that he had a walnut allergy, what precautions would Burton St Clair have taken to safeguard his health in the event of his inadvertently eating something contaminated with walnut?'

'I assume he would have had an EpiPen.'

'A what?' asked Detective Sergeant Knight

Jude wasn't sure whether he was feigning ignorance to prompt some indiscretion on her part, so she replied in a level voice, 'An EpiPen is an adrenaline auto-injector which is used by allergy sufferers to counteract the effects of anaphylactic shock.'

'You seem to know a lot about them. Did you know Burton St Clair always carried one?' asked Knight eagerly.

But Jude wasn't going to be caught in such a simple trap. 'No, I didn't know that. But for someone with an allergy like his, carrying an EpiPen would have been a normal precautionary procedure. And the reason that I "seem to know a lot about them" is that in my work as a healer I come across a lot of clients with allergies. And most of them carry an EpiPen.'

'Hm. Thank you, Jude.' The Inspector's use of her first name was accompanied by a manufactured smile. 'Could we move on, please, to talk about your relationship with Burton St Clair . . .?'

'Of course. But nothing has changed since we last spoke.'

'I would still like to ask you a few more questions.'

'Very well, Inspector.' Meekness did not come naturally to Jude, but she knew that was what her current circumstances required.

'When we last spoke, I had not then spoken to Megan Sinclair.'

'I remember. The call from her came while you were here.'

'Exactly. So I am now in a better position to check what you tell me with the evidence that she provided.'

'Yes, but I would point out that Megan's recollection of things could be inaccurate.'

'I will, of course, take that into account.'

'I mean, she was wrong about my knowledge of Al's walnut allergy, so she might—'

'Yes, thank you.'

'If you could allow the Inspector to ask her questions without interruption, that would be very helpful, Jude.' Knight looked across to his superior for approval of his intervention. He didn't get any.

'Jude,' said Rollins, 'when we last spoke, you told us that you and Burton St Clair had never had a romantic or sexual relationship.'

'That's as true now as it was when I said it before.'

'But you don't deny that he "came on" to you in his car on Tuesday night?'

'No, I don't deny that. That is what happened.'

'But why, having not seen you for "fifteen . . . twenty years"? I believe that was the time-scale you suggested?'

'Yes. Nearer fifteen. He and Megan got married twenty years ago. It was round the time of their divorce that I stopped seeing them.'

'Thank you for clarifying that. Why would Burton St Clair suddenly "come on" to you, if there had never been any previous relationship between you?'

'Because that was the kind of man he was. He regarded himself as fatally attractive to women. Every woman he met was a challenge to him. Surely you've met men like that, Inspector?'

'I don't think my experiences are really relevant in this situation.'

'Very well. All I'm saying is that, whatever woman had got into his car, Burton would have made a pass at her.'

'And you know this . . . why?' asked the Detective Sergeant. 'Because he had made passes at you on previous occasions?'

'Yes.'

'But you had never responded to them? Never agreed to take things further?'

'Never, Sergeant.'

'Well, here again,' said Rollins, once again looking down at the screen, 'we have a discrepancy between your recollection of events and Megan Sinclair's.'

'Do we?' asked Jude wearily.

'When we spoke to her on Wednesday afternoon, she told us that you and her husband had started an affair very soon after you first met him.'

'Did she?' In the Kafkaesque situation where Jude found herself, there seemed very little point in making further protest.

'Megan Sinclair said it was your relationship with her husband that broke up their marriage.'

Jude knew her friend had always been mentally unstable, but hadn't realized it had gone that far. Was it really possible that

Megan believed the fabrications which she had elaborated during her years of loneliness?

Or worse – a new thought invaded Jude's mind – was it a case of deliberate lying? Had Megan made these accusations against her former friend in revenge for some imagined slight?

'It is a pity, Inspector,' she said bleakly, 'that Burton St Clair is no longer alive. He could at least have corroborated my story that the two of us never had an affair, however much he may have wished for such an outcome.'

'I wouldn't be so sure of that, Jude.'

'Oh?'

The Detective Inspector's expression was implacable. 'According to Megan Sinclair, it was her husband who told her about the affair you'd been having.'

Jude's reserve finally broke. 'Then he was lying!' she burst out. 'Either Burton lied or Megan lied.'

'Yes.' Rollins smiled grimly. 'There is, of course, a third possibility, Jude. And that is that you lied.'

ELEVEN

Carole was unused to seeing her neighbour in the state she was that morning. As soon as the police left, Jude had rushed round to High Tor, and was now being comforted with coffee in its hospital-clean kitchen. Carole's Labrador, Gulliver, snuffled comatose sympathy from his cosy station in front of the Aga.

And Jude, a woman whose healing brought ease to her many clients, was the one in need of healing.

'I mean, it's ridiculous, Carole. All I did was resist Al's advances, leave him in his car and walk home in the rain. Now suddenly it seems that I'm the police's Number One Suspect for having murdered him.'

'Resisted *whose* advances?'

'Sorry, there's a lot you don't know about this.'

'That is certainly true.' There was an edge of resentment in Carole's words. Jude felt a momentary sting of guilt. Surely her neighbour couldn't know about her mini-betrayal of conducting investigations with Oliver Parsons?

She dismissed that for the stupid thought it was. But it was a reflection of her emotional instability that she had given it a moment's brain-room.

'Well, Carole, the first thing to mention is that the police say they are investigating a murder.'

'So . . .' Her neighbour smiled with satisfaction. 'For once the Fethering consensus has proved accurate.'

Jude then went on to relive every moment of the two police interrogations. This inevitably provoked a little frostiness in Carole. The first interview with the police had, after all, taken place on the Wednesday morning, but Jude had then divulged nothing about the encounter over their cottage cheese lunch at High Tor. Carole, always quick to detect a slight, was beginning to feel marginalized.

The other information Jude had to pass on did nothing to improve the atmosphere between them. She could not avoid filling in the history of her friendship with Megan and its broadening into a threesome when Al Sinclair appeared on the scene. Nor could Jude not mention Megan's conviction that she and Al had had an affair.

Predictably, this was the detail Carole picked up on. Over the years, Jude had had a varied sex-life, but it had never been as lurid as it was in her neighbour's imagination. 'So, you're saying positively that you didn't have an affair with him?'

'Absolutely positively, definitely not! I do know who I've had affairs with.'

A beady look came into Carole's pale blue eyes, as though she doubted this assertion. 'Then why would Burton St Clair have told his wife that he had had an affair with you?'

'Because that was the kind of man he was. He thought he was irresistible to women. He must have claimed me as yet another of his conquests.'

'I still don't see why he'd do that. When would he have told her?'

'I don't know every detail, do I? It was probably in the course of some marital row. He saw a way of needling her. Maybe she'd expressed some jealousy of me.'

'Why would she do that . . . if there was nothing to be jealous of?'

'Just take my word for it! Al may have fancied me, but – absolutely! definitively! – nothing ever happened!'

'So you admit that he fancied you?'

Jude was finding this hard work. Carole seemed at least as sceptical as Rollins and Knight had been. She pursued the point. 'But if nothing ever happened, why was Megan so convinced that something had happened?'

'Because she was paranoid. Because the fantasy of Al and me having an affair had somehow in her mind been converted into truth.'

'And the police believed Megan about the affair?'

'Yes, she's convinced them.'

'But why would she do that – and why would they believe her – if it wasn't true?'

'Carole, will you please stop going round the same bloody questions!' Jude never swore. Her use of the word was another indicator of the stress she was under.

'Of course,' said her neighbour, 'there could be another reason for Megan to insist on her account of things . . .'

'Yes,' said Jude wearily.

'She might have pushed the suspicion towards you to cover her own tracks.'

'Sorry?'

'Megan Sinclair would need the police to have another prime suspect . . . if she herself had committed the murder!'

Carole sat back triumphantly, and Jude recognized that this line of thought was preferable to herself being cast in the role of prime suspect.

'From what you say,' her friend went on, 'Megan Sinclair had plenty of reasons to hate her ex-husband. She would certainly have known about his walnut allergy. And she—'

Jude had to stop her. 'I like the way you're thinking, Carole. Sadly, though, there is no way Megan could be linked to the scene of the crime at Fethering Library on Tuesday evening.

She was visiting a friend, another former actress, in Scarborough. The police have checked that out.'

'Well, maybe she put some walnut into a sandwich which she knew Burton was likely to eat when he got in the car after his talk and she . . .' Carole's speculations trickled away in the face of Jude's shaking head. 'Just a thought,' she concluded lamely.

'Anyway, when I was with Megan, she told me—'

'You didn't say you'd seen her.'

'Didn't I?'

'No. I assumed everything you said about her came from what the police told you.'

'Sorry you got that impression. I had lunch with Megan on Thursday.'

'Did you? So, you were investigating the murder on your own?'

This wasn't going well, from Jude's point of view. 'No,' she replied patiently. 'At that stage the police hadn't used the word "murder". And I wasn't *investigating* with Megan. I was just trying to find out whether she knew anything more than I did about her ex-husband's death.'

'So far as I'm concerned, that comes under the definition of "investigating".'

Jude hadn't got much fight left in her. 'Very well. If you like.'

'And may I ask where your investigations are leading you next?'

'Steve Chasen seems to be the next obvious port of call.'

'Steve who?'

'Steve Chasen. He was at the library on the Tuesday night, generally making a nuisance of himself, and Oliver Parsons has managed to get a contact for—'

'Sorry? Who is Oliver Parsons?'

'He's someone else who was at Burton St Clair's talk.'

'Someone you knew before?'

'No. Just someone I met that evening, and he and I were talking about Burton's death . . .'

'Were you?' The expression on Carole's face told Jude that she was just digging herself deeper and deeper in.

'And, as I say, Oliver's got this contact for Steve Chasen, and I was thinking . . .' She tried to get herself out of the situation. 'It would be very good to have you on board in this investigation, because now it's not just curiosity. I'm genuinely worried the police are going to try to pin this on me. And, if they do, I guess I could be arrested, and then I'd need you to find out what really happened and . . .'

'Oh, I don't think you'd need *me*,' said Carole. 'I'm sure your new friend Oliver Parsons could solve the case for you.'

'What I'm saying is that, when we go and talk to Steve Chasen, you should come along too, to catch up on the details of the case.' There was a note of pleading in Jude's last few words.

'Oh, no,' said her neighbour frostily. 'I wouldn't want to *intrude*.'

Sometimes Carole Seddon was just *so* Carole Seddon.

TWELVE

Steve Chasen, it turned out, worked as a night shelf-stacker at a big Sainsbury's in the retail park outside Clincham, 'which brings in a bit of loot and gives me time to write.' He did the weekends, Friday, Saturday and Sunday nights – 'better hourly rate.' He clearly wasn't keen for them to come to his home, and when Oliver Parsons had suggested that they meet in the Crown & Anchor early that evening, he didn't like that idea either. 'Not a good idea to drink when I got a night shift coming up. And I'm one of those people who can't go into a pub and not have a bevvy.'

So instead, that Friday evening at six, Jude and Oliver met him at the relatively new Starbucks, in what used to be Polly's Cake Shop, on Fethering Parade.

Compared to how he had been on the Tuesday night, Steve Chasen was very definitely on his best behaviour. Though still dressed in his uniform of various camouflage patterns and Doc Martens, he showed none of the aggression he had demonstrated at the library.

'I saw you at the talk,' he said with something approaching charm, 'but we didn't get a chance to say much.'

'No.'

'So, until Oliver mentioned it on the phone this morning, I didn't realize that you were an agent.'

Oh dear, Jude had completely forgotten the cover stories which had made Steve agree to a meeting. Though she had done a little acting in her time, she really didn't relish playing a part for the whole evening. Also, if Steve Chasen lived locally, he would very soon find out her real identity. Besides, Jude's inherent honesty would not allow her to raise his hopes about the possibility of his science-fiction novel ever being published.

She had to get out of the situation with the minimum amount of lying. 'I'm sorry,' she improvised wildly, 'Oliver must've misunderstood me. I'm not a literary agent, I'm a *healing* agent.'

She was worried this made her sound like some kind of antiseptic cream, but Steve didn't seem to read it that way. Nor, on the other hand, did he seem very pleased by what she'd said. Looking accusingly at Oliver, he demanded, 'Then why the hell did you set up this meeting?'

Smooth as ever, the former television director tried telling the truth. 'We're just interested in what happened at Fethering Library on Tuesday night.'

'All right, I got pissed,' said Steve Chasen, his aggression returning with a vengeance. 'What the hell business is that of yours?'

'It isn't our business, but—'

'Then why the hell are you wasting my time?' He stood up, ready to walk out.

But Oliver Parsons' next words stopped him. 'We aren't wasting your time. We're talking to you because the police are now treating the death of Burton St Clair as murder. And on Tuesday evening you were heard in front of a lot of witnesses threatening and badmouthing him.'

Slowly Steve Chasen sank back into his chair.

'Have the police been in touch with you?' asked Jude. She nearly added 'yet', but she thought that would be overdoing things.

'I had a message on my mobile,' Steve mumbled. 'I haven't got back to them.'

'They'll keep trying,' said Oliver.

'Well, yes,' Steve conceded. 'Presumably, if they think it's murder, they'll want to talk to everyone who was at the library on Tuesday night.'

'Yes, everyone,' Oliver agreed. And then, perhaps unfairly, he added, 'But they'll want to speak to some people more than others.'

'Meaning me?'

Oliver shrugged, as if the answer to Steve's question were self-evident. The younger man coloured. 'But I haven't got anything to do with murdering anyone.'

'I'm sure you haven't. Nor has Jude. But the police have talked to her, and given her quite a rough ride, so we thought we could probably help prepare you for when they do talk to you.'

Jude had to admire the way he'd brought the argument round, so that now it seemed they were supporting Steve Chasen, rather than just picking his brains.

The younger man nodded. 'OK. Well, like I said, on Tuesday at the library I just got pissed. That's all. And all right, the guy got up my nose, but I certainly didn't murder him.'

'We're not suggesting you did,' Jude reassured him. 'But if we share our recollections of what happened that evening, then we'll be better placed to knock down any suspicions the police may have about us.'

'Yes, I can see that,' Steve Chasen agreed slowly.

'First thing we ought to clear up,' said Oliver, 'is whether you had had any previous dealings with Burton St Clair? Had you met him before?'

Jude detected a moment's hesitation before Steve replied, 'No. He just represented everything I hate about a certain type of writing. Making it to the bestsellers with some middle-class, menopausal romance . . . Don't know what his bloody book's called, but I know what I think of it.' He made a retching sound. 'God, that's not what writing should be about – not about ordinary people doing bloody ordinary things. Writing should involve imagination. Books shouldn't copy life, they should create life.'

'Like yours do?' Jude suggested.

'Yes, exactly like mine do. All right, I know I haven't had
the success that some useless tosser like Burton St Clair
has had, but in time my books will be recognized for what
they are.'

Jude didn't think it was the moment to point out the
ambiguity of what he had just said, but Oliver asked, 'You
mean, your work might be discovered posthumously? Like
Gerard Manley Hopkins?'

Steve Chasen looked puzzled. 'Don't think I know him. Did
he write science fiction?'

Leaving his question unanswered, Jude moved the conversation in another direction. 'The police say that what killed
Burton St Clair was an allergic reaction to walnuts. Did you
know that?'

'No, of course I bloody didn't. You've only just told me he
was murdered.'

'Did you know he was allergic to walnuts?'

If this was an attempt by Oliver Parsons to wrong-foot Steve
into an admission he had met Burton St Clair before, it didn't
work. 'No,' came the reply. 'Of course I didn't. I told you,
I never met the guy.'

'Well,' said Jude, 'the police seem to think that someone who
did know about his allergy managed to get some walnut – I
don't know, ground walnuts, chopped walnuts, walnut essence
– into something Burton drank at the library that evening. It
seems unlikely anything could have been got into a sealed water
bottle, but the bottle of red wine that was open in the staff
room . . . well, that might be more feasible.'

'We know that you went into the staff room, Steve,' said
Oliver, 'I imagine to get more drink at the end of the evening . . .'

'All right, what if I did? I didn't go in there with a pocketful
of chopped walnuts, I can assure you.'

'We're not suggesting you did,' said Jude soothingly, 'but
we just wanted to know what you saw when you were in there.'

'What kind of thing?'

'Well, was there a bottle of red wine by the sink?'

'Yes.'

'A full bottle?' asked Oliver.

'Yes.'

'With its screw-top off?'

'Yes.'

'So, what did you do with it?'

'What do you think I did with it? I went in there with an empty glass because I wanted a drink.'

'You poured yourself one?' asked Jude.

'No. I would have done, but then that interfering librarian came in and stopped me. She said I couldn't have any more, because the speaker hadn't had a drink yet.'

'And she poured a glass for him?' asked Oliver.

'Yes.'

'Was it just Di with you in the staff room?'

'No, that sidekick of hers, grumpy kid who was running the bar.'

'Vix Winter,' said Jude.

'I don't know her name. She was the one who kept trying to stop me topping my glass up in the actual library.'

'So, what happened after Di had poured the glass for Burton?'

'Well, there was still three-quarters of a bottle left, so I reckoned I was due a top-up and I reached for the bottle, but both the girls reached for it at the same time and it got knocked over and smashed on the floor. Which I thought was a bloody waste of good red wine . . . well, not that good red wine, but still a waste.'

Jude and Oliver exchanged looks, both thinking the same thing: that if the walnut – in ground form or whatever – had been put in the wine bottle, seeing that it got smashed might be a good way of destroying the evidence, after Burton's glassful had been poured. Jude remembered Vix Winter telling Di Thompson that she'd tidy up the mess.

'So,' said Oliver, 'assuming you didn't put the walnut into the wine bottle, Steve—'

'Which I bloody well didn't!'

'We should think who else might have had the opportunity to do it. In other words, who else went into the staff room that evening.'

'Well, all right, I'll hold my hand up,' said Jude. 'I went through to the Ladies at the end of Burton's talk, so I had an opportunity to do it. An opportunity which, as it turns out, I didn't take.'

'There was quite a lot of traffic to the loos,' said Oliver.

'So any one of the old biddies of Fethering could have doctored the drink,' suggested Steve sarcastically. 'Out of thwarted love for the author of *Stray Leaves in Autumn* perhaps . . .?'

That revealed that, despite his earlier avowal, Steve knew full well what Burton's book was called. Indeed, he would have had to be pathologically unobservant to have sat through the entire Tuesday evening in Fethering Library without knowing. Jude wondered if there were other, more relevant, details of which he claimed ignorance. Everything about Steve Chasen's manner and body language suggested to her that he was hiding something.

She caught Oliver Parsons' eye. His expression implied that he didn't think they were going to get any more useful information out of their interviewee.

So they left Steve Chasen to the excitements of his night shift at Sainsbury's in Clincham. And asked him to let them know if he had any contact from the police.

He wasn't the first person on the police contact list, though.

Jude had considered asking Oliver in for a drink, but when the Range Rover drew up outside Woodside Cottage, there was another vehicle parked outside. A Panda car. Detective Inspector Rollins and Detective Sergeant Knight emerged from it to welcome her home.

'Would it help if I were to come in?' suggested Oliver Parsons.

'No. Thank you, but no.'

'There are quite a few things that interest us about your behaviour,' said the Inspector.

'Oh?'

They were once again on the sofa and chairs of the front room at Woodside Cottage. Never before had three bottoms perched so unrelaxedly on their welcoming contours.

'For instance,' Rollins went on, 'we find it interesting that you feel the need to be in contact with potential witnesses of events in the library on Tuesday . . .'

Jude offered no more than another 'Oh.'

'Particularly since these contacts follow on from your meeting with Megan Sinclair on Thursday.' This time Jude was silent. 'So, on Thursday evening you contact Oliver Parsons who, so far as we know, you had not met before the Tuesday.'

'No, I hadn't. And, incidentally, I didn't contact him. He contacted me.'

'Of course,' said Rollins, clearly disbelieving. 'Then this evening you both go and talk to Steve Chasen.'

Jude had always known there were few secrets in Fethering. Once the police became involved, it seemed there were absolutely no secrets in Fethering.

'So why do you find this odd behaviour?' asked Jude.

Detective Sergeant Knight took it upon himself to answer that one. 'The Inspector means that your actions would seem to show an excessive interest on your part in the details of Burton St Clair's death, almost as if you were trying to find out how much other people know about the circumstances of that death – which actions could be construed as guilty behaviour.'

For the first time, Rollins did not express disapproval of her junior's intervention. Jude wondered whether this implied some collusion between the two detectives, some prior planning as to how they were going to conduct this latest interview.

'For someone in my situation,' said Jude calmly, 'your approach seems calculated to make me feel guilty.'

'What exactly do you mean by that?' asked Rollins.

'You're behaving as though you think I had some connection with Burton's death.'

The Inspector did not deny this. Instead, she came up with some standard police verbiage. 'We're at a very early stage of our enquiries, Jude. We haven't ruled out any possibilities. We're just trying to gather as much information as we can about the background to the case.'

'So are you saying I am not on your list of suspects?'

'I am not saying that, no.'

'Are you denying that I am your Number One Suspect?'

The Inspector's brow wrinkled with distaste. 'I'm afraid expressions like "Number One Suspect" tend not to be used outside the confines of television police dramas.'

'Let me put it another way then. Am I high up on your list of suspects?'

'I'm afraid, until we have solid evidence that will remove you from that list, you will remain there.'

'But it should be obvious that I had nothing to do with it.'

'Obvious to you, maybe. Perhaps less obvious to us. Listen, Jude, when we investigate a crime, we start off with almost no information. We don't know the place where the offence happened, we don't know the people involved. So we start gathering information – and that's something we're very good at. We have much more experience than the average *amateur*.' She slightly leant, with a hint of criticism, on the last word. 'And the information we gather leads us towards certain hypotheses as to what might actually have happened. So, if a lot of facts that we get together seem to point in a certain direction, we follow the logic through until we find a new fact which renders that particular hypothesis invalid. In this case, we have yet to find the fact that makes our current hypothesis invalid.'

'Your current hypothesis being that I murdered Burton St Clair?'

'I didn't say that, Jude. It's not our habit to share the details of our investigations with people who might be significant witnesses.'

'Or who might be the perpetrator of the crime?'

'I didn't say that either.'

'No, but the implication was there.'

The Detective Inspector shrugged. 'What you infer is up to you.'

From her relish for language, Jude was getting the firm impression that Rollins must have been a fast-track graduate entrant to the police force – perhaps another cause of disharmony between her and the Detective Sergeant.

But it wasn't the moment for such sociological observations. 'So what you're looking for, Inspector,' she asked, 'is a piece of evidence that would rule me out as a suspect in this case?'

'That would be enormously helpful,' Rollins replied, 'both to us and to you.' But she couldn't resist adding, 'If such a piece of evidence exists.'

Jude was silent.

'Look at it from our point of view,' the Inspector went on. 'We know the cause of Burton St Clair's death. We think it likely that chopped walnut, ground walnut – something containing walnuts – was put into the bottle of red wine in the staff room at Fethering Library. We know you were aware of the deceased's allergy to walnuts.'

'You only have Megan Sinclair's word for that.'

'We also only have Megan Sinclair's word for the fact that your affair with her husband broke up their marriage.'

'And I keep telling you that that affair never happened.' Jude was beginning to lose her cool.

'Megan seems convinced it did. And why should she make it up? Has she any reason for wanting to get you into trouble?'

'I don't know. Megan is . . . mentally very confused. She seems to have convinced herself that the affair did happen, so in her mind it did.'

'Just in her mind?'

'Yes!'

'Very well. Then we come on to your recent behaviour. If you had nothing to do with the crime, why have you been going round contacting witnesses?'

'Well, obviously, to find that vital piece of information, evidence, whatever, that will convince you I had nothing to do with it! Don't you believe me?'

'Yes, of course.' said the Inspector, who clearly didn't.

Jude felt she was up against a brick wall. 'Look,' she asked, as near to despairing as her positive nature ever allowed her to get, 'short of getting a confession out of me – which you're not going to get; I am not in the habit of confessing to crimes I didn't commit – what would be the next stage of your investigation, so far as I'm concerned?'

Rollins looked thoughtful. 'Well, if we can't get any more useful information from you, and we don't get any new information out of any of the other witnesses—'

'People like Steve Chasen? He said he hasn't spoken to you yet.'

'We left a message for him. We'll get round to him in time.'

'So, apart from talking to people like him, what would your next step be?'

'I suppose at some point we would apply for a warrant to search your premises.'

'To search here? To search Woodside Cottage?'

'Yes.'

Somehow this news, more than anything else that had been said, made Jude realize how seriously she was being taken as a suspect. 'And then – what? If you can find some chopped walnuts in my kitchen, that's it? I must have committed the murder?'

'I'm not sure that—'

'Go on then!' Jude was up on her feet, gesturing towards the kitchen door. 'Have a look! See what you can find! Do it now, why not? There's no time like the present!'

There was a silence. The two detectives looked nervously at each other, not quite sure how to take the invitation that had been presented to them.

'Well, don't hang about,' said Jude. 'It's a good offer. Detective Sergeant Knight, I guess this might be your territory. Why don't you search my kitchen while the Detective Inspector keeps an eye on me to see that I don't try to escape?'

'Well . . .' Knight looked again at Rollins. 'We don't actually have a search warrant.'

'You don't need a search warrant, do you,' demanded Jude, 'if I've given you my permission?'

She appealed to the Detective Inspector, who nodded and gestured the Detective Sergeant to go into the kitchen. As he went through, Knight pulled a pair of rubber gloves out of his pocket. And put them on.

'Good,' said Jude. 'Let's get this thing sorted out, shall we? Now, while he's doing that, is there anything else you wanted to ask me?'

Rollins had recovered her equilibrium by now. 'Not so much what I want to ask you, but perhaps a few things I should tell you.'

'Yes?'

'Whatever happens next, I think you would be very ill-advised to continue to pursue your own investigations into Burton St Clair's death.'

'Oh no!' Jude clutched both hands to her ample bosom. 'This

happens in every television cop show I've ever seen. I've been taken off the case!'

Perhaps unsurprisingly, Detective Inspector Rollins did not see the humorous side of this response. She continued as if nothing had been said. 'I obviously cannot give you orders as to who you should or should not talk to, but your making contact with other potential witnesses might give the impression that you were trying to influence the testimony that they give.'

'Yes, fine, I get the point. But, Inspector, please tell me you can at least understand why I want to make contact with such people.'

Rollins looked more po-faced than ever. 'No, I can't really understand that.'

'For heaven's sake!' Jude was getting really rattled now. 'To clear my name! To find some evidence which proves that I have nothing to do with Burton St Clair's death! I just want to get at the truth!'

'Exactly what we want to do, Jude. But I think we might get to the truth more quickly if you stopped withholding information.'

'I am not withholding information! And I haven't lied to you either. I just come back to the same thing. How many more times do I have to say it? I had nothing to do with the death of Burton St Clair!'

Jude saw the Inspector's gaze move towards the kitchen. She turned. Detective Sergeant Knight standing in the open doorway. Between finger and thumb of his gloved right hand he held the neck of a bottle.

'I found this, Inspector. It's walnut oil.'

THIRTEEN

'It's the *huile de noix* I bought when I was in Périgord last summer,' said Jude. 'I'd forgotten I'd got it.'

'"Forgotten I'd got it"?' Detective Inspector Rollins echoed sceptically.

'Yes, I was doing a week's Mindfulness Workshop.' Rollins's expression suggested that Mindfulness Workshops weren't high on her list of priorities. 'There were a lot of other healers of various disciplines there, and there was one who was raving on about the health benefits of *huile de noix*. I mean, it's full of Omega-3 fatty acids, supposed to be good for lowering blood pressure and reversing the hardening of blood vessels. Some people also use it in the treatment of eczema.'

Detective Sergeant Knight looked down at the bottle he was holding. 'This is only about half full. Some of it's been used.'

'I wanted to test whether it did have any beneficial effects, so I tried it out on some of my clients. I'm always open to testing different kinds of therapy.'

'Good,' said Detective Inspector Rollins drily.

From somewhere the Sergeant had produced an evidence bag, into which he placed the bottle of oil.

His superior rose from her seat. 'I don't think we need trouble you any further this evening, Jude.' And though she didn't actually emphasize the words 'this evening', the implication was clear that there would be further 'troubling' at some future date. 'But I would just like to reiterate that your continuing to contact people who might have relevant information about Burton St Clair's death will not help your cause.'

'"Cause",' Jude repeated. 'Are you sure you don't mean "case"?'

'I don't understand what you're saying.'

'What I am saying, Inspector, is that you seem to be building up such a strong case against me as the murderer of Burton St Clair, I'm surprised you don't arrest me right now and get it over with.'

'We don't have enough evidence to make any arrest at this point,' Rollins replied primly. 'Good night. We can see ourselves out.'

Carole Seddon was not used to hearing her doorbell ring after eight o'clock at night. In common with most of the residents of Fethering, unless she had planned to go out for an evening or, much more rarely, invited someone to visit her, the drawbridge of High Tor was firmly up as soon as Gulliver had had his final walk.

So that Friday evening she approached the front door with some trepidation. The sensor light over the porch had come on, but she had no idea who her visitor was. She unlocked the door, but kept the chain in place, and squinted through the narrow aperture. 'Who is it?' she asked, in a voice which sounded much bolder than she felt.

'It's me, Jude, for heaven's sake!'

Even though they were neighbours, such unannounced visitations between them were rare. As she unhooked the chain, Carole asked, 'Can I get you a cup of coffee?'

'No,' said Jude. 'Open a bottle of wine.'

They drank in the kitchen, as usual. Carole's front room was rarely used. Though it contained its share of padded upholstery, there was an antiseptic chill about the place. The kitchen, though kept as scrupulously clean as an operating theatre, did at least have the Aga to generate some level of cosiness. In front of it, Gulliver sighed and grunted, deep into some dream of chasing seagulls on Fethering Beach.

'So,' said Carole, when they were settled with their glasses of New Zealand Sauvignon Blanc, 'you seriously think you are the police's prime suspect?'

'Increasingly, that's the way it looks.'

'Walnut oil seems a strange thing to have in one's kitchen.'

'Carole, for heaven's sake! You remember when I went on that course last summer . . .'

'Oh yes, the mindlessness thing . . .' This was as near as Carole Seddon ever got to making a joke. She was always having a go at her neighbour's beliefs in alternative medicine, and it was not the first time she had made this particular gibe.

'Mind*ful*ness, as you know full well,' said Jude wearily. 'Anyway, that was in Périgord, which is the walnut centre of the universe. Every shop sells the stuff, and it does have medicinal properties, so I thought I'd try it.'

'Hm. Still seems a strange thing to have in one's kitchen.'

'Well, it was there, and I'd used some a few months back for a client with serious eczema.'

'And did it work?'

'No, it didn't seem to improve her condition.'

Carole sniffed, as only she could sniff. 'There are, of course, treatments for eczema available in conventional medicine.'

'I know that,' said Jude, unwilling to re-engage with Carole's scepticism about her profession. 'But listen, the most important thing is that Detective Inspector Rollins has warned me off doing any further investigation of the case.'

'Well, you can see her point,' said Carole, going all stuffy and Home Office.

'But the situation's changed. The case needs investigating more than ever – simply to prove that I didn't murder Al.'

'Why are you telling me all this?' asked Carole, deliberately obtuse.

'Because if I'm not being allowed to find evidence which proves that I didn't commit the murder, someone else is going to have to find it!'

There was a silence. Then, as if she'd just been jolted awake, Carole said, 'Oh, you mean me?'

'Yes, of course I mean you!'

Carole was secretly delighted. One of her favourite dreams was coming true. The idea that Jude, habitually so serene and in control, should be asking for her help was a very attractive proposition. But it wasn't in Carole's nature to express her delight outwardly.

'Oh,' she said, as if dubious. 'Well, you'll have to give me all the background . . .'

'Yes, of course.'

'. . . but then I might be prepared to bring my mind to bear upon the problem.'

'If you would,' Jude pleaded.

Carole glowed inwardly. Always worried about being marginalized in the investigations she and Jude had undertaken, here she was being offered the starring role. But she didn't want to show how much the situation appealed to her, so all she said was a gruff, 'All right, I'll give it a go.'

'Thank you so much. And, Carole, as I mentioned, I've been talking to Oliver Parsons about the case. He was there on Tuesday night, and he has lots of good ideas. I'll give you his mobile number.'

'Do, by all means.' Not that Carole had any intention of ever ringing it. The only person she conducted investigations with was Jude. And since Jude was going to be unavailable for this one, Carole Seddon was determined to solve it on her own.

FOURTEEN

A few years before, Carole would have known nothing of what went on in Fethering Library. But, thanks to the enrolment of her granddaughter, it had become a familiar venue for her. And Carole herself had become a sufficiently familiar face for her to be greeted by name when she arrived there the following day.

The greeter that Saturday morning was Eveline Ollerenshaw, who was standing by the issue desk, performing some vague function Di Thompson had invented to give her the illusion of usefulness. (Evvie didn't actually check the books out; that was now done automatically.)

'Carole, how nice to see you. Not got Lily with you then?'

'Not today.'

'Because you often bring her on Saturdays. For all the children's activities.' The noise level in the library indicated that those activities had already started.

'Yes, I sometimes do. But she's with her parents in London today.'

'Nice for you to have her sometimes, though, isn't it?'

'Oh, yes.'

'And of course she's got a little sister now, hasn't she? Remind me what her name is?'

'Chloe.'

'Lovely names, both of them. Of course, I didn't have kiddies myself. Gerald and I had hoped that one day . . . but it just didn't happen. I suppose—'

Carole was not in the mood for one of Evvie's monologues. 'Is Di about?' she asked crisply.

'Oh, she was over by the . . .' The old woman looked across

the library and, just at that moment, Di Thompson emerged from the staff room, pushing a trolley. Carole made a fairly polite escape from Eveline Ollerenshaw, and greeted the librarian.

'Haven't seen you for a while, Carole,' said Di Thompson. Her dark hair looked even shorter in the daylight. On the sloping shelves of her trolley, rows of books stood up like bricks on a builder's hod. She started to check through them as she too observed, 'No Lily?'

'Not with me today.'

'Ah. Well, as you see, she's missing the usual Saturday morning chaos.' Di gestured across to the children's section, from where enough noise emanated to destroy forever that cartoon image of librarians always having fingers to their lips and saying, 'Ssh.' Children of all sizes, monitored by parents lying uncomfortably on the floor or perched on tiny chairs, scampered about. One or two sat unmoving, immersed in their storybooks. Others were being encouraged by a couple of twenty year olds to make face masks out of paper plates. The white surfaces were decorated with scribbles in coloured crayon, stickers and bits of post-Christmas tinsel attached by glue-stick.

'They seem to be having fun,' Carole observed.

'Oh yes. Do you mean the kids or the grown-ups?'

'Both.'

They looked across. The twenty year olds had both donned masks and were improvising some kind of slapstick routine which their junior audience was finding hysterical.

Carole grinned. 'Were such activities part of the job description when those two applied to become librarians?'

'They're not librarians. Sadly, I haven't got enough staff to do that kind of thing. We can just about manage running the children's story-time sessions on Wednesdays, but otherwise we have to rely on volunteers – God bless them.'

'Ah.'

'People like Evvie.'

Di Thompson didn't put any critical intonation into her words, but Carole knew exactly what was meant. 'Ah,' she said.

The librarian pointed back to the children's area. 'Those two deserve some kind of sainthood, or a medal at the very least. Both primary school teachers. Not content with spending their working weeks corralling the little bastards, they actually volunteer to come here and do more of the same on their Saturday mornings.'

'You're lucky to have them.'

'You can say that again.' All the time she was talking, the librarian was working, picking up books from the trolley, checking them through and, according to their condition, placing them on one or other of the lower shelves. 'Without my volunteers and my part-timers,' she went on, 'this place'd close even sooner than it will do anyway.'

'Is it going to close?' asked Carole.

Di Thompson shrugged. 'Wouldn't surprise me. Government cuts are hitting all the local amenities. And libraries are currently in a pretty vulnerable state. Borrowings down, people find it so easy to read e-books or order real books on Amazon. Then kids spend all their time playing computer games rather than reading, people who used to rely on the library for computer services seem mostly now to have their own laptops or tablets. The reference information we used to provide is all available at the touch of a button from Wikipedia . . . I could go on. The effects of all that are already being felt – even here in West Sussex. In other parts of the country there are a lot of libraries reducing their opening hours, stopping their mobile library services, some closing down completely. And a few continuing as community libraries, all run by volunteers. It's not a great time for us.'

'But libraries are part of our heritage,' said Carole piously. 'There are people whose entire education has come from their public library. Surely they can't be allowed just to disappear? Somebody must do something about it.'

'What, though? And, more importantly, who? Who's going to do something about it?' Di Thompson looked Carole straight in the eye. 'It's the old "use it or lose it" syndrome. And I often wonder whether the people who do say how terrible it is, who write letters to the papers saying we mustn't lose our libraries, saying that an efficient library service is an essential part of a civilized society – do they actually use their local branch as much as they should?'

Carole looked away. She didn't know whether Di was actually getting at her or not, but she still felt guilty.

'We keep trying to drum up more interest in this place, but it's an uphill struggle. Special events, all that . . .'

'Library talks?' Carole suggested, seeing a way of getting to the subject she really wanted to talk about.

'Oh, yes,' said Di. 'They can be quite popular, but the trouble is, it's always the same people who attend. The Fethering stalwarts, mostly female, mostly over seventy. Very loyal, but as they die off, who's going to replace them? What I do these days is rather similar to being a vicar, watching my congregation slowly slipping away to nothing.' As she spoke, her hands were still busily sorting the books.

Carole decided to take the direct approach. 'And does a library talk attract more interest if the evening ends in a murder?'

Di Thompson let out a small, sharp laugh. 'Well, it would appear to, yes. Certainly had more people joining the library this week than we have had for some time. I think that's maybe something to do with them wanting to visit the scene of the crime.'

'And was this the scene of the crime?' asked Carole.

It had been a half-hearted attempt to see whether Di might reveal that she knew more detail about Burton St Clair's death than the rest of Fethering. As such, it failed. The librarian replied, 'The scene of the crime was actually in the car park. I'm surprised you hadn't heard that.'

Carole covered up. 'Oh, there's been so much gossip in Fethering during the last week, it's hard to pick out the truth from the speculation.'

'Tell me about it.' Di Thompson let out a jaded sigh. 'I've heard more theories about whodunit than you'd find in the entire crime section.'

'Any convincing ones?' asked Carole hopefully.

'No. Each one sillier than the next.' The librarian gave her a sharp look. 'Why, are you about to inflict yet another one on me?'

Carole had been offered an opening, and she knew she had to use it with caution. 'Well, I was talking about it with

Jude, my neighbour, you know, who was here on Tuesday night . . .'

'I know Jude.'

'. . . and the police had spoken to her . . .'

'Detective Inspector Rollins and her sidekick?'

'Yes.'

'I have sympathy for her. They've taken up a lot of my time this week.' She gestured to her trolley. 'Otherwise I wouldn't be sorting out this lot on a Saturday.'

'Jude said the police told her Burton St Clair was killed by anaphylactic shock after eating something containing walnuts, to which he was allergic.'

Di Thompson looked at her with new respect, realizing she was dealing with a Fethering resident who actually knew some of the facts in the case. Which was quite a novelty. 'Yes, that's what they told me. And I had to close the library on Thursday while they searched the place. Kept the staff room shut up yesterday too. Which was very inconvenient, because they gave me so little notice about it.'

'Presumably,' said Carole, hoping to channel the librarian's resentment of the police towards further revelations, 'they checked the staff room where the wine had been kept for drinks after Burton St Clair's talk?'

'Yes. Looking for traces of walnuts, I suppose.'

'And did they find any?'

That was greeted by a cynical laugh. 'Well, if they did, they weren't going to tell me about it, were they?'

'Of course not.' Carole knew all too well how reticent the police could be when it came to sharing their findings with amateurs. 'You were actually there when the bottle was broken?'

'Yes.'

'From what Jude said, you'd poured a glass for Burton St Clair from the last remaining bottle in the staff room?'

'That's right.'

'And then when Steve Chasen went to pour a glass for himself, you reached out to stop him and that's how the bottle got knocked over?'

'Yes. Vix Winter, my junior librarian, was there too.'

Carole looked around the room. 'Is she here today?'

'No. She should be.' There was a lot of resentment in Di's voice. 'She called in sick.'

'Are you suggesting she's not sick?'

'I just think, for a girl of her age, she suffers from a remarkable amount of illness.'

'Right.' That, clearly, was an ongoing staffing problem which did not concern Carole. 'So, going back to the bottle getting smashed, it could be any one of the three of you who knocked it over?'

'I suppose so. But it wasn't deliberate. It was an accident.'

'But if it had been deliberate, any one of you could have ensured that it fell on to the floor?'

'Perhaps, but why would we want to?'

'To destroy the evidence that chopped walnut had been infiltrated into the bottle?'

'Oh, I see, right. Well, I can assure you, Carole, I haven't been infiltrating chopped walnut anywhere.'

'I wasn't suggesting you had been.'

'No? You are aware, aren't you, that you and Jude have got a bit of a reputation around Fethering for seeing yourselves as amateur sleuths?'

'Have we?' asked Carole innocently.

'Very definitely. Why else do you think I'm answering your questions?'

'Oh.' Carole felt her face colouring. 'That's very kind of you.'

'Anyway, I didn't like that Detective Inspector Rollins's attitude. If anyone's going to solve the case, I'd much rather it was the local amateurs.'

'That's also very kind of you.'

For the first time that morning, there was a twinkle in the librarian's eye as she said, 'I think I've been spending too much time in the crime section. I'm afraid I'm a sucker for those Golden Age books in which the baffled PC Plods have rings run round them by brilliant amateurs.'

'Does this mean you're giving me *carte blanche* to ask as many questions as I wish?'

'Mm.' Di pointed down to the few remaining books on the top shelf of her trolley. 'Not too many. When I've finished this lot, I must go and once again engage with the public.'

'Fine. Just a few quick questions then. Jude got the impression that the remains of the broken bottle in the staff room had been cleaned up by your junior?'

'Vix, yes.'

'Do you know how she did it?'

'I asked her that. She told me she got some kitchen roll and picked up the larger bits of glass with that over her fingers, so that she didn't cut herself. She put those in the pedal bin by the sink. She swept up the smaller shards with a dustpan and brush, and put them in the bin too. Then she mopped up the wine and remaining tiny bits of glass and washed the mop out under the tap over the sink.'

'The dustpan, mop and what-have-you . . . where were they kept?'

'There's a broom cupboard just next to the staff toilets. When she'd finished, Vix put everything back in there.'

'And was the pedal bin emptied subsequently?'

'It would normally have been. That's part of the cleaners' duties. They come in at nine, but only two days a week. Their next day would have been Thursday, but of course with the library being closed . . .'

'So the police have presumably got the remains of the wine bottle?'

'They'll be pretty inefficient if they haven't. No sign of the pedal bin contents this morning. Nor, come to that, of the dustpan and mop from the broom cupboard. Which is another inconvenience.'

'Taken away for forensic analysis?'

'Assume so. That's what happens in all the television police shows, doesn't it? So they can be examined by some guest star playing a scientist way out on the extreme edge of the Asperger's spectrum.'

Carole grinned. Behind her quiet exterior, Di Thompson was a sharp and highly intelligent woman.

'So soon the police will have proof that it was walnut extract in the wine bottle that killed Burton St Clair?'

The librarian shrugged. 'That would seem to be the logical conclusion. But, as I said before, I doubt if that's data they're likely to share with us.'

She looked down at her watch, but before she had time to say anything, Carole got her oar in. 'Steve Chasen . . .'

'Yes?'

'According to Jude, he was badmouthing Burton St Clair after his talk.'

'True enough.'

'And he would have had a chance to put something in the wine bottle?'

'I don't know. I wasn't watching his movements all evening.'

'But he could have deliberately ensured that the wine bottle got smashed?'

'I suppose he could.' The librarian sounded reluctant to accept the suggestion. 'I'm sorry. I know Steve's a pain, and on more than one occasion I've had to ban him from the library, but there is something about him I respect.'

'Oh?'

'Well, I know he gets pretty unmanageable when he's been drinking, but he's completely self-taught. He's one of those people who's got all of his education from the public library.'

'An autodidact?'

'Yes, the exact word. And not one that's heard very often these days. Nor do we get a lot of people in the library these days, *educating* themselves. Most now seem to learn stuff from YouTube videos. So, though I can't condone a lot of Steve's behaviour, I do think he's one of those people for whom the library service was set up and, I fear, one of a dying breed.'

'Admirable,' said Carole crisply. 'But, of course, that doesn't rule out the possibility that he's also a murderer.'

'No, I'll concede that.'

'And what about your junior – Vix Winter, is it?'

Di Thompson's face tightened up. It seemed that her junior was not the most co-operative of colleagues. 'What, do I think she's a possible murderer? I can't see it. Planning something like that would be too much like hard work.'

'Ah. Would you have a contact number for her?'

Di provided it. 'But I wouldn't try her today. Remember she's *ill*.' The last word was loaded with a wealth of cynicism.

'Thanks, anyway. Ooh, one other thing . . .'

A weary 'Mm?'

'I've been trying to contact other people who were here for Burton St Clair's talk. Jude mentioned some tall American woman, who was something of an expert on crime fiction?

'Nessa Perks. Possibly Professor Nessa Perks. Don't know what her proper title is, but she's involved in the English Department at the University of Clincham. She helped out on a few sessions for the library's Writers' Group.'

'Oh yes, Oliver Parsons mentioned that.'

'Mm. He used to come along for a while. Mind you, we don't run it any more.'

'Funding?'

'Partly. More lack of interest from the good people of Fethering. Same problem that's scuppered a good few other initiatives I've set up to prove the relevance of this library in the twenty-first century. Book group's still running, but the rest of them . . .'

With an air of finality, Di Thompson moved the last book from her trolley's top shelf to a lower one. 'There. I must—'

'Just one more question.'

'Yes.' There was now a put-upon edge to the librarian's voice.

'Jude said that when Burton St Clair put his arm round you, you flinched.'

'I don't deny it.'

'Any particular reason? Or just general dislike of men you don't know well putting their arms around you?'

'Well, there was more of a reason with Burton St Clair. The bastard had just come on to me in the staff room.'

'Really?'

'Yes, pushing me against the wall, one hand on my breasts, the other up my skirt. I had to fight him off.'

'I'm sorry.'

'Not the first time it's happened with an author. A lot of them seem to have some feeling of entitlement when it comes to groping librarians. And groping members of their publishers' publicity departments, come to that. One of the clichés of publishing life, I believe – authors having it off with publicity girls.'

'Oh? Then, if he came on to you, you did have a strong reason to dislike Burton St Clair?'

'Yes,' said Di, with a sardonic look at Carole. 'What I didn't have, though, was time between his groping me and my getting him a glass of wine, to research the fact that he had a walnut allergy, to source some chopped walnuts, and to infiltrate them into the bottle of red wine in the staff room.'

'I can see that,' said Carole, feeling a little put down.

'Now I'm afraid I have—' A cacophony of infantile screaming had suddenly broken out in the children's section. The two twenty year olds in paper-plate masks were faffing around, clearly not up to resolving the situation. Carole saw two toddlers locked in a boxer's clinch, bawling and pulling each other's hair out. Worse than that, the two toddlers' dads were also squaring up to each other.

'I must go and sort things out,' said the librarian.

FIFTEEN

V ix Winter seemed surprisingly ready to talk to Carole. About anything. When told it was about Burton St Clair's death, she was even more enthusiastic. And no, she hadn't had any face-to-face conversations with the police yet, just a call in which she'd been asked to confirm that she had left the library in Di Thompson's car on the Tuesday night. She'd been questioned briefly about cleaning up the staff room when the bottle of wine had been broken, then told that the police would probably be contacting her again at a later date. But, since then, she hadn't heard anything more from them. She sounded disappointed, and Carole wondered whether that's why she'd agreed so readily to talk to her.

'We can't do it here, though,' the girl whispered conspiratorially down the phone line. 'I live with my parents.'

'Well, when do you think you'll be well enough to meet up?'

'What?'

'I've just come from the library. Di Thompson said you'd called in sick.'

'Oh yes. Actually, I'm feeling a bit better than I was earlier. Thank goodness. Could meet now if it's OK with you?'

'Fine. Where?'

'I don't know. Some pub?'

'My local's the Crown & Anchor in Fethering. Don't know if you know it?'

''Course I do. I've lived in the village all my life.'

'Whereabouts?'

'Downside.'

'Right.' Carole had duly taken note of this social marker. The Downside Estate, to the north of Fethering, was made up of council houses – or, as they seemed to have become known, 'social housing'. Their world was far from the middle-class gentility of High Tor.

'Then of course you know the Crown & Anchor. Well, might that be suitable? Or would you worry about meeting Di there – you know, what with you being off sick?'

'That'd be OK. She never goes near the pub. Doesn't drink.'

'So, when could you meet?'

'I don't know . . . twelve?'

'Sounds good to me. What, will you walk there, or do you have transport?'

'Ooh, no. Couldn't afford a car on my salary. But I don't really fancy walking, not with being off sick and all.'

'Of course not. I'll pick you up then.'

Carole's instructions were not to collect the girl from the house. She was to pick Vix up by the postbox at the end of her road. Whether the girl wanted the assignation to be a secret from her parents, or was ashamed of where she lived, Carole neither knew nor asked.

So, the immaculate Renault was driven sedately out of the High Tor garage. For a moment, Carole considered telling Jude what was happening, even suggesting she might come along. But she curbed the instinct. Her neighbour seemed to have been genuinely frightened by the cautions Detective Inspector Rollins had given her. Jude wanted to – indeed, had to – keep her nose clean.

Which meant that Carole Seddon was the sole investigator on the case, if you didn't take the police into account. And, despite her Home Office background, when Carole was involved in an investigation, she very rarely took the police into account.

Vix Winter hadn't said much on the short drive from Downside, and she didn't say much inside the Crown & Anchor until she had taken a long swig from her pint of cider. As instructed, Carole had asked at the bar for a 'K' (which was apparently some kind of cider), but Zosia had said they didn't carry it, so she had made do with draught Aspall's.

Carole hoped Ted Crisp didn't appear in the bar. The sight of her in the company of a girl with green hair and facial piercings would provide him with teasing ammunition for weeks.

'Phew!' said Vix, putting her glass down on the table. 'I needed that.'

'Oh?' said Carole, after taking a sip from her small Sauvignon Blanc.

'Got a bit bladdered last night.' She took her mobile phone out and placed it on the table right in front of her. 'On the "K", I was, with my mate Jools, in this club we go to.'

'And then you woke up this morning feeling ill?'

'Yes.' A sly grin crept across the girl's plump face. 'Don't know why.'

The temptation for Carole to be censorious was only momentary. She was reminded that she needed to ingratiate herself with Vix Winter to extract the maximum amount of information from the girl.

'You presumably know about everything that happened after you left the library on Tuesday evening?'

'Well, I don't know *everything*, or I'd know who the murderer is, wouldn't I?' She giggled, and took another long, revivifying swallow from her pint glass. 'But I know what I saw, sure enough. Everyone in the library's been asking me about it, and at the club we were in last night too.'

She spoke with some level of pride. Vix Winter wasn't the first person Carole had encountered who glowed in the spotlight turned on them by having some involvement in a murder enquiry.

'Right, on the Tuesday, after the library had been locked up, Di Thompson drove you home?'

'Yes.'

'Was that a usual arrangement?'

'How'dja mean?'

'Did Di normally give you a lift home, if you both finished work at the same time?'

'God, no. She could do that quite easily, I'm virtually on her way, but she'd never think of it. No, normally I have to walk, or catch a bus. But, as I'm sure you know, there's no buses in Fethering at that time of night.'

Carole nodded agreement, although, thanks to her trusty Renault, she had not travelled by bus once since she had moved permanently to the village.

'On Tuesday, Di had to promise me a lift home. Otherwise there was no way I was going to stay for the evening. I thought it was a liberty asking me to do it, anyway. No talk of overtime. I know the hours I'm meant to work, and evenings aren't part of them. Having spent the whole day dealing with books, last thing I want to do is stay at work in the evening for some bloody author.'

It wasn't the first time during their interview that Carole had contemplated asking Vix whether she thought she'd really taken the right career path. Though there were not many librarians amongst her acquaintance, the ones Carole did know were very devoted to their profession. They might moan about management and changes in regulations, as everyone who worked for a large organization did, but they did actually care about the libraries and the customers who frequented them. Above all, they loved books.

But that was a part of the job specification which seemed to have passed by Vix Winter.

'Tell me,' asked Carole, 'did Di say anything about the evening as she was driving you home?'

'No. She hardly said a word. Except "Goodnight" when she dropped me at the end of our road.'

'She didn't make any comment about Burton St Clair? Or the contents of his talk?'

'No.'

'What did you think of it?'

'What did I think of what?'

'Burton St Clair's talk.'

'I don't know.'

'Well, you were there, weren't you? You must've heard what he said.'

'I wasn't listening. I was sat at the back with my mobile. Spent most of the time WhatsApping my mate Jools.'

Once again, a question about Vix's suitability for her chosen career was on the tip of Carole's tongue. But she didn't let it go any further than that. 'Presumably you were in the library when Burton St Clair arrived that afternoon?'

'Yes, he got there about six. Library closed at five thirty, so Di and I had had to rush around moving chairs and things before he arrived.'

'I gather some volunteers were there too, to help put the chairs out?'

'Yes. But I did most of it.'

'And what time were the doors opened for the public?'

'Six thirty.'

'Did you get the impression that Di had met Burton St Clair before?'

'Don't think so. She went into her routine about how much she'd always enjoyed his work, and how delighted she was about the success of . . . whatever the new one's called. But I've heard her do all that with other authors.'

'Hm. Earlier, Vix, you talked about the "murderer". Has anyone actually said that Burton St Clair's death was murder?'

'Well, everyone in Fethering says it was.'

'But you haven't heard the word used by the police?'

'Like I said, I only had a brief chat on the phone with them.'

'Of course. When Burton St Clair did his talk, I understand he had a bottle of mineral water with him . . .'

'Oh, are you going down the poisoning route? Yeah, a lot of people have been talking about that. And before you ask: no, the bottle of water had not been opened before it was set up for him. I know that, because I took it out of the staff room fridge myself.'

This did of course raise the possibility that Vix herself might have had the opportunity to adulterate the contents, but Carole didn't think that avenue was worth pursuing. She was coming round to Di Thompson's view that planning a murder would have been too much like hard work for Vix Winter to have anything to do with it.

'God, I feel better for that.' Vix looked down at her empty glass. Carole took the hint. Though she was only halfway down her Sauvignon Blanc, she went to the bar to get another pint of Aspall's. Zosia served her. The girl looked rather subdued and, Carole noticed, wore heavier eye make-up than usual. The whites of her eyes were pinkish, as though she'd been crying. Jude would instantly, without any awkwardness, have asked Zosia if everything was OK. But Carole wasn't made like that. She just voiced her thanks and took Vix's cider back to the table.

As the girl took another deep swallow, Carole asked, 'Do you mind just going through what happened between Burton St Clair's arrival at the library and the start of his talk?'

'Not much did happen, really. I told you, I spent most of the time moving chairs.' The resentment in her voice was strong. 'Some volunteers were meant to come in at six thirty to help with that, but by the time they arrived I'd done it all,' she concluded righteously.

'And where was Burton during this time?'

'He was in the staff room with Di. She'd got some M & S sandwiches. Not that I was allowed to have any. They were all for him. And she made him some coffee.'

'Didn't offer him anything stronger at that stage of the evening?'

'No. She was worried about not having enough wine for later.'

Carole remembered Jude saying Burton had had a close relationship with alcohol. 'Did he mind about that?'

Vix shrugged. 'I don't know. I didn't hear him say anything.'

'So, Di was in the staff room with him, what, talking about his books?'

'I guess,' said the girl without interest.

Carole changed direction. 'Was Burton St Clair wearing an overcoat when he arrived at the library?'

'No. He was parked directly outside. Maybe he'd got one in his car.'

'I think Jude said he was wearing a black leather jacket.'

'That's right. But when he was chatting with Di, he took it off and hung it over the back of the chair.'

'You don't know how long it stayed there?'

'I don't think he picked it up again before he went through to the library for Di to introduce him, you know, at the beginning of his talk.'

'So there might have been a moment when the jacket was left unattended in the staff room?'

Another shrug. 'Might have been. Quite likely, I suppose.'

'One other thing. While he was in the library on Tuesday, did Burton St Clair make a pass at you?'

'"Make a pass"? What you mean, like, "come on to me"?'

'Yes.'

'No, he bloody didn't!' The girl looked disgusted to the depths of her dumpy soul. 'He's *old*.'

'Were you aware that he had "come on" to Di Thompson?'

'To Di?' Her nose wrinkled with further distaste. 'Oh my God, that must've made her day.'

'I don't think it did.'

'Well, I think it's a long time since she's seen any action of that kind. I can't imagine her ever doing it, actually.' The pierced nose was wrinkled with disgust. 'Her and Burton St Clair – yuk!'

'Well, apparently he did grope her.'

'That's horrible.'

'Why?'

'Well, they're both so *old*!'

To Carole Seddon, who was probably exactly the same age as Di Thompson, this was less than amusing. 'There was one other thing I wanted to ask you, Vix. About the timing of—'

She was interrupted by a pinging from the girl's phone. Without a word of apology, it was picked up. A text was read, and a short reply sent off.

'Sorry, gotta go. My mate Jools is outside in her car. We're going on to meet some people in another pub.'

And, pausing only to down the remains of her cider, Vix Winter rushed out of the Crown & Anchor.

On her way to the door, Carole did the public-spirited thing of taking the two empty glasses up to the bar. Zosia was slumped forward against it, looking even more dejected.

'Are you all right?' Carole asked, knowing that Jude would have put the question less brusquely.

She was right. The Polish girl looked up. Tears started to sparkle on the heavy mascara of her eyelashes, and she went wordlessly out through the door that led to the kitchen.

'Women's moods, eh?' It was the landlord, Ted Crisp, barrelling his way along the bar towards Carole. 'Though presumably saying that would be sexist these days, wouldn't it?'

'Probably. Though I didn't think political correctness had ever really been your thing, Ted.'

'Well, it certainly wasn't so important when I was doing the stand-up circuit. Nowadays, almost any joke you make is going to offend some minority. No way round it, though, so far as I can see. Jokes have to be at *someone*'s expense, for heaven's sake. Jokes have to have butts, otherwise they're not jokes.'

'Maybe.' Carole found Ted's company obscurely comforting. The fact that they had once had a brief affair was still a source of surprise to both of them. Though the differences in their personalities meant that a relationship of such closeness could never have lasted, it had remained a bond between them.

She moved on. 'Do you know what's wrong with Zosia?'

He shrugged awkwardly. 'Moods?'

At least he hadn't said 'time of the month', thought Carole, though she knew exactly what he meant. She was constantly amazed by how embarrassed men got about the subject of periods. And how they assumed that they must be the cause of all of women's emotional upsets.

'Let me fill your glass up.'

'No, Ted, I should really be—'

'On the house.'

She didn't argue.

He poured out the New Zealand Sauvignon Blanc and pulled himself half a pint of Sussex Gold. This was unusual. Though

Ted Crisp liked to build up the image of himself as a hard drinker, it was increasingly rare for him to sample his own wares. He had seen too many pub landlords ruin themselves and their businesses by sliding down the easy slope to alcoholism.

Anyway, trade was slack. Even though it was a Saturday, pubs across the country were still suffering from the post-Christmas slump. He raised his glass to his guest.

After they had toasted each other, Carole suddenly remembered that Jude had entrusted her with a murder investigation, and one in which Ted might be able to provide more information. 'People still talking about that business with Burton St Clair in the library?'

'Of course they are. It only happened on Tuesday and, in case you've forgotten, we do live in Fethering, a village where a dog fouling the dunes can fuel six months' worth of gossip. No way they're going to stop talking about a murder in four days, is there?'

'No. When Jude and I were last in here, you talked about some American woman pontificating in here with some theories about different kinds of murders.'

'Yes, I remember her. At the time, I thought what she was saying was a load of cobblers, and I haven't changed my mind on that.'

'You don't know if her name was Nessa Perks, do you?'

Ted shook his head. 'No idea what she was called.'

'And you don't know if she had any connection with the University of Clincham, do you?'

His eyes lit up. 'Oh yes, I do remember one of the kids she was with mentioning the place.'

'Thank you.' At least Carole now knew who was the next person she should try to contact.

As, feeling rather mellow, Carole walked back from the pub to High Tor, for the first time she wondered whether Jude might actually have had something to do with Burton St Clair's death. The thought was quickly suppressed, but she knew it was one which, once planted, would continue to linger just below the level of her consciousness.

SIXTEEN

Jude couldn't get away from the feeling that she was under house arrest. Detective Inspector Rollins had only warned her off continuing her private investigation, but it was as if a hold had been put on all other areas of her life. Going shopping, going out for a walk: nothing felt right.

She even postponed a couple of healing sessions she had booked over the weekend. This was unusual. The needs of her clients always took priority over her own concerns. But she knew that, in her current emotional state, she would not have the focus required to channel her healing powers.

Nor did her vast repertoire of therapeutic resources help. Though she knew a multitude of ways to bring peace to the troubled souls of others, nothing seemed to mitigate her own uneasiness. The biblical proverb, 'Physician, heal thyself', was a difficult instruction to follow. Physicians have never been particularly good at applying their expertise to themselves.

It was very out of character for Jude to be in such a twitchy state. But, as the sequence of coincidences – culminating in the discovery of the *huile de noix* bottle – continued, she felt herself getting deeper and deeper into some Kafkaesque nightmare which could only end in her arrest.

Of course, the one link in Rollins's chain of condemnation which Jude knew to be untrue was her supposed affair with Burton St Clair. It didn't really matter whether Megan had affirmed its existence from sheer vindictiveness, or because a jealous suspicion in her paranoid mind had over the years hardened into fact. The accusation had been made, and the Detective Inspector believed it.

For a moment Jude contemplated ringing Megan, trying to reason with her, persuading her to rescind the statement she had given to the police. But she quickly rejected the idea. For a start, Megan was probably convinced that the lie she had told was the truth. And, looking at the situation from the police perspective, if Jude were guilty of the murder, then it would be entirely logical for her to put pressure on their star witness to change her story. Doing that wouldn't help her cause one iota. No, every avenue Jude considered following appeared to be blocked.

And she couldn't really blame the police for the direction in which their suspicions were moving. There was a logic there. Was it possible that she was the victim of some elaborate plan to frame her? Why? And who would do such a thing? It wasn't an idea to make her tangled thoughts any clearer.

For the first time, she wondered whether she ought to contact a solicitor. At one level, it was insane she was even contemplating such a step. On the other hand though, even if Rollins hadn't actually voiced the threat, she would clearly love to see Jude in court. If professional help was going to be required, perhaps she should start doing something about it?

The telephone rang. Hearing Oliver Parsons' voice at the other end of the line did nothing to diminish Jude's confusion.

'Just wondering how your interview with the police went yesterday?'

God, was it only yesterday? Jude had been through so much emotional turmoil since Oliver had dropped her home it seemed like an age ago.

'I'm afraid I can't really talk about it.'

'Oh? That doesn't sound like you, Jude.'

'No, it isn't like me. The fact is, Oliver, the police have told me that I mustn't investigate any further.'

'Have they? Worried that the amateur sleuth might solve the murder before they do?'

'You've been reading too many of your Golden Age crime novels. No, they have just told me to back off.'

'They reckon you're interfering with their enquiries?'

'Something like that.'

'Does this mean they're near to a solution of the crime? Do they have a prime suspect?'

'They have. And I'm afraid it's me.'

'What?' He sounded genuinely gobsmacked. 'Are you serious?'

'I'm afraid I am.'

'My God. And are they still thinking that Burton St Clair was killed by some walnut extract in the wine bottle?'

'Yes. Well, I haven't heard to the contrary.'

'I was going to suggest meeting up for a . . . I don't know . . . a drink or a—'

'No. Sorry, Oliver. But until I get the police off my back, I don't feel like socializing.'

'Oh. Well, that's fine. I'll give you a call in a few days.'

She wondered whether he would. Had she choked him off too prematurely? She felt a little wistful. There had definitely been a spark between them; something might have developed.

But the potential end of an embryonic relationship was the least of Jude's worries.

Any normal neighbour – obviously in the more relaxed North of England, but even in the frostily genteel South – would have knocked on the door of Woodside Cottage when walking past. But not Carole Seddon. Even after so many years of friendship, from the Crown & Anchor she went back to High Tor, then rang Jude from there and asked if she could call round.

Her neighbour was still jumpy. Jude's paranoia was not decreasing. She was worried that her phone was tapped and that she was permanently under surveillance. Maybe Detective Inspector Rollins and her team were also now checking Carole's movements and would extend to her the ban on investigating Burton St Clair's death.

Jude expressed this anxiety, but her neighbour just said briskly, 'If that is the case, then I should bring you up to date with what I've found out as quickly as possible.' And she delivered a characteristically efficient report on her interviews with the two librarians and Ted Crisp.

The detail that Jude clung on to was that the remains of the wine bottle had been taken off for forensic analysis. 'If they don't find any evidence of walnut contamination – or if they find it didn't come from *huile de noix* – then that'll finally prove I couldn't have had anything to do with the murder.'

Carole did not look convinced. 'You're still apparently the last person to have seen Burton St Clair alive. I'm not sure that the police will drop you off their list of suspects straight away.'

'Thanks,' said Jude ironically.

'Anyway,' Carole continued, determined as ever, 'until I actually am warned off by the police, I intend to go on with this investigation.'

'So, what will be your next step?'

'I'll try to make contact with this Nessa Perks woman. I'm not sure whether she'll have anything useful to contribute, but at least she's another witness to the events of Tuesday night.'

'Do you have a number for her?'

'No, I'll have to go through the University of Clincham. Though whether there'll be anyone around there at the weekend, I don't know.'

'Good luck.'

'Don't worry, Jude. I'll sort this out. There's no way I'm going to let you get a life sentence for a crime you didn't commit.'

To Jude this sounded a little over-dramatic. But it did address the basic source of her anxiety. And to know that she had Carole fighting her corner was very comforting.

It was about half-past five when the telephone next rang in Woodside Cottage. 'Hi, Jude, it's Zosia.'

'How lovely to hear you.' But Jude recognized the tension in her voice. She remembered from her last visit to the Crown & Anchor how down the girl had been looking. 'Everything all right?'

'Yes,' Zosia replied instinctively, but her tone told another story.

'Are you sure?'

'No, I am not sure.' After dedicated study and classes, she now spoke perfectly grammatical English. But her accent remained, and grew thicker when she was in an emotional state.

'Is it something you can talk about?'

'Yes. It is something normally I would have talked to Tadeusz about, but obviously I cannot do that.' The pain caused by her brother's death did not go away.

'If talking to me would help . . .'

'Please. I like to. But not on telephone. I need to see you to talk.'

'That's fine. Would you like me to come to the pub?'

'No. Saturday night it is already filling up. We are booked out for dinner. It will be a busy evening.'

'Well, tell me when you'd like me to come.'

'Please, it is easier if I come to you. Tomorrow morning? I do not have to be on duty till twelve.'

'Fine. You remember where Woodside Cottage is, don't you?'

'Yes, of course.'

'Say ten thirty?'

When she put the phone down, Jude felt a warm glow. It would be good to concentrate on someone else's problems for a while.

And if she was under police surveillance, they couldn't object to her being visited by Zosia. The girl had nothing to do with Burton St Clair's murder.

SEVENTEEN

Carole reckoned she'd done everything she could to get in touch with Nessa Perks. Without any personal contact, she could only make an approach through the University of Clincham website. She went to the Creative Writing degree course section and discovered that her quarry was listed as 'Professor Vanessa Perks'. This confirmed a trend Carole had spotted. Every professor interviewed on Radio 4's *Today* programme nowadays seemed to be female and American.

No direct email addresses for any of the teaching staff were listed, so Carole sent a message to the English and Creative Writing Department, marked 'FAO Professor Vanessa Perks'. Whether it would reach its destination, and how long it would take to reach that destination, she had no means of knowing.

It was frustrating not to be able to move her investigation on more proactively, but she reconciled herself to the fact that there would probably be no reaction from the University of Clincham at a weekend. So, the highlight of Carole's Sunday would have to be a Skype conversation with her granddaughter Lily in Fulham. (Initially wary of all new technology, but manically enthusiastic once she had embraced it, Carole had now become a devotee of Skype.) And though she wished she saw more of

Lily and her younger sister Chloe in the flesh, she did relish engaging on the screen with her older granddaughter's increasing articulacy.

Zosia arrived at exactly ten thirty. When she took off her fur-lined parka, she revealed her work uniform of white shirt and black trousers. Her make-up and pigtails were perfect and Jude was struck by how pretty she was. She can't have lacked for interest from the young men of Fethering but, so far as Jude knew, she hadn't had a boyfriend since she'd been working at the Crown & Anchor. Maybe the hours of a bar manager weren't conducive to an active social life, but Jude reckoned the girl's single state was more a result of the long mourning process she was going through for her murdered brother.

Once they were both supplied with coffee, Jude asked directly, 'What's the problem?'

'It is my uncle Pawel. My mother's brother.'

Jude didn't know that Zosia had an uncle, but made no comment. She could recognize when someone needed to talk, and let the girl run on.

'He has come to England only six months ago. He had much unhappiness in Poland. He lost his job. My mother thought he might have more chance of getting another job here in England, but it is not easy. Uncle Pawel is maybe sixty-five years old; it is as hard for him to get a job in England as it was in Poland.'

'What's his profession?'

'I don't think you would call it a profession; it is a job. In Poland he was a builder. Not a builder who runs projects, just a building labourer. So now he is old, although he would never admit it, he does not have the strength for the heavy work any more. That is why he lost his job in Poland. And it is the same here. Even if he were English, he would not get a labouring job here.'

'"Even if he were English"?' Jude echoed.

'You know what I mean.'

'You mean that there is prejudice in this country against the Polish?'

'Of course. If you work in a pub, you hear a lot of it.'

'I'm sorry. I thought you were quite settled here.'

'I am, yes. And I have good friends, and I know many people who do not care what country I come from. But in the pub, you know, there are many Polish jokes.'

'Jokes about the Poles being stupid?'

'Yes, yes, of course.' Zosia dismissed the subject. 'It doesn't worry me now. Maybe it would worry me, if I thought I *was* stupid.'

'You are far from stupid.'

'I know this. So for me it is sometimes an irritation, but not a problem. For Uncle Pawel, whose English is not so good, the problem is bigger.'

'Where does he live?'

The girl grimaced. 'Since he has been in England, he has lived with me. He sleeps on a sofa bed in my sitting room.'

'That doesn't sound ideal.'

'No, it is not, Jude, but it is how it has to be, at the moment. He is family. He is my mother's brother.' The way she spoke suggested that she had never questioned the obligation such a relationship placed on her.

'Of course. So, is that what the problem is: finding somewhere else for him to live?'

Zosia sighed. 'That is part of the problem. Only a small part.' She took a deep breath, preparing herself for the next section of her narrative. 'The fact is, Jude, that Uncle Pawel has always had a problem with alcohol. In Poland too, yes, the vodka. But when he was working, it was fine. Yes, he drank a lot, but the physical work kept him fit. He never turned up late, he never failed to do his work. It was not a problem for his boss, it was a problem for his family.'

'Is he married?'

'*Was* married,' Zosia replied glumly. 'Finally, his wife could not put up with the drinking, so she left. Now they are divorced. He had become violent, you see, which is not in his nature. Uncle Pawel is a gentle, simple man, until he gets the vodka inside him. Then he changes, you know, like Jekyll and Hyde.'

Jude was impressed by the girl's command of British literature, as she went on, 'I have tried to stop him drinking, but it is no good. He does not want to stop. At first he thought that, because he has a niece who works in a pub, that will be a source of free drinks for him. I pretty soon stopped him thinking on those lines. Now he is banned from the pub. But there are plenty of other places you can get alcohol.'

'Legally?'

That prompted another grimace. 'I worry about that. With Uncle Pawel, the dependency is so strong, he is quite capable of stealing from an off-licence, or stealing money to buy alcohol. And so, to stop him from doing this, I give him money, though I know exactly what he will spend it on.'

'I see your problem.'

'And the terrible thing is, Uncle Pawel is bad for the Polish community here on the South Coast. We are mostly hard-working people, and we have managed to put up with the prejudice and live alongside the locals in a friendly way. Then someone like Uncle Pawel comes along, and all the lines about "bone-idle immigrants, taking advantage of our welfare system" – well, they become true. And Uncle Pawel is not alone. There are a few – very few, I am glad to say – like him. And they gravitate together. He finds other Polish layabouts to drink with. They hang about in the shelters on the seafront, drinking together. People see them, hear they are speaking a foreign language. It is not good for the image of the Poles.

'And then some of the men Uncle Pawel drinks with are into drugs, too. It is easy to get drugs round here – Littlehampton, Bognor; you don't even have to go to Brighton.'

'And does your uncle use drugs?'

'I do not know for sure, but I think it is likely,' came the bleak response.

'Hm. Zosia, you spoke of "taking advantage of our welfare system". Does that mean you've consulted health professionals, alcohol recovery programmes, about your uncle's problems?' If not, Jude could certainly help. She had a comprehensive list of such services at her fingertips. It was surprising how many of her clients, even in nice, middle-class Fethering, had dependency issues.

Zosia blushed. 'No, it is . . . I do not want to ask for outside help. Uncle Pawel is family. My mother would not like me to make his shame public.'

Jude was beginning to realize the extent of the girl's troubles.

It was more than someone of her age should have to cope with. Then suddenly she had another thought, a memory of her walk earlier that week to Fethering Library.

'Zosia, you said your uncle and his drinking mates often got together in seafront shelters?'

'Yes?'

'You wouldn't remember whether he was out drinking last Tuesday evening?'

The girl's brow wrinkled. 'I'm not sure.'

'It was the evening that ended up with the writer's body being found in the library car park . . . well, no, it was actually the following morning that the body was found, but—'

'I know what you are talking about. It's been the main topic of conversation in the pub all week.'

'I bet it has. Anyway, as I was walking along the front last Tuesday, on my way to the library, about half-past six I suppose it would have been, I heard some people carousing in one of the shelters on—'

'No, that would not have been Uncle Pawel,' said Zosia firmly. 'Tuesday is my day off at the pub. So that Tuesday evening I cook for him. Good Polish food. *Kopytku* he likes very much, like my mother cooks, like their mother cooked for them when they were children. That night he does not drink. And he is the Uncle Pawel I have always known and loved.'

'And then on Wednesday he's back to his drinking ways.'

'Usually, yes.'

'But not this week?'

'I do not know. That is why I am so worried, so upset. Uncle Pawel has disappeared.'

EIGHTEEN

Carole, who hadn't expected any contact to be made till Monday at the earliest, was surprised to get a call back from Nessa Perks on the Sunday morning. The Professor was in her office at the University of Clincham. 'Research is an ongoing project,' said the American. 'It doesn't stop just because of a weekend. The weekdays get so cluttered up with teaching, often the weekends are the only time I can concentrate.'

Carole explained that she would like to talk about the events of the Tuesday evening, 'because I gather you were present then at Fethering Library.'

'Yes, I was,' Nessa confirmed.

'Have the police talked to you about anything you might have seen?'

'No, they haven't.' The Professor was clearly piqued by this official shortcoming. 'You would have thought they would have done, knowing that I am an internationally recognized expert on crime.'

Carole didn't raise the question of how the police might have been expected to know that. Instead she said, 'I thought your expertise was in fictional rather than real-life crime.'

'You'd be surprised how frequently the two correlate,' Nessa Perks replied. 'They are, not to put too fine a point on it, inseparable. In fact, that is the basis of the research I am currently doing for a new book.'

'That sounds very interesting,' said Carole, though something in the Professor's manner suggested to her that it wouldn't be. 'Anyway, I was wondering if we could meet to talk about Burton St Clair's death?

Professor Vanessa Perks was very keen on the idea. Miffed by the apparent lack of interest from the official enquiry, she was more than ready to share her theories with anyone who'd listen.

The agreed time was four o'clock, by which time the day was colder than ever. The lethargic gatekeeper at the university's main entrance had been alerted to Carole's arrival and directed her towards the English and Creative Writing Department. Then he returned to his electric fire and *Fast and Furious* DVD. Drawing close, as instructed, she rang the Professor's mobile to announce her arrival, and was admitted through a door protected from intruders by a keypad code.

The willowy Nessa Perks said little until she was actually in her office, and when they got there, Carole could see why. The Professor wanted to impress all visitors with the magnificent contents of her shelves. For there, in serried ranks, stood a huge array of old books. All crime novels. The hardbacks looked to date from the Twenties and Thirties, and Carole recognized the green and white livery of the Penguin paperbacks.

She was obviously expected to say something on the lines of 'You've got quite a collection there', so that was exactly what she said.

'Yes, fairly comprehensive. Probably as good a collection as there is in this country, outside of specialist libraries.'

'And are they all yours?'

'Well, technically the university purchased them, but I curated the collection.'

Carole had noticed that in contemporary life more and more people seemed to be 'curating' all kinds of things, but she supposed curating a collection of books was closer to the original meaning of the word than some other of its many current usages. She also got the firm impression that if the University of Clincham ever wanted to claim back the books they had bought for Professor Vanessa Perks, they might encounter a problem. When she looked at her shelves it was with a proprietorial air.

Though Carole didn't realize it, the Professor represented a relatively new trend in academia, whereby genre fiction was given serious intellectual scrutiny. Thirty years before, the idea of university students studying crime or science fiction would have been laughable, but they had both become serious academic disciplines. Like many, the trend had started in America, but quickly been embraced by British universities. (There were even course notes available, which summarized the plots of Agatha Christie novels for students who found the effort of reading them too challenging.) And people like Professor Vanessa Perks were riding the crest of this new wave.

The academic was dressed that morning in an over-frilly cream blouse, a thin black skirt that came down to mid-thigh and Victorian buttoned boots. Her make-up was so immaculate that it looked almost as if there were a transparent shell over her face. The china in which she served tea from a silver pot

was crinkled around the edges. Carole got the impression that
the Professor was one of those Americans who was a little too
fervently in favour of all things British. The tea, inevitably, was
Earl Grey.

Before Carole had a chance to issue any prompt, Nessa Perks
was straight into her lecture. 'As I mentioned on the telephone,
many people too readily dismiss any possible correlation
between Golden Age mystery fiction and the real-life world of
contemporary crime. But my extensive researches into the
subject have revealed that many of the tropes occurrent in
the whodunits of the time can act as relevant comparators.

'And that is certainly true in the case of Burton St Clair's
death. When broken down into their essential components, in
such crimes certain patterns obtain. This kind of murder is
almost always domestic, and it always starts with the husband
having an affair. Then there are three possible scenarios that
can happen. For ease of memorizing them, I refer to the scenarios
as "HKW", "WKM" and "WAMKH".'

Carole didn't think it was appropriate to say that she had
already had this routine spelled out by Ted Crisp. But she
admired how efficiently the Professor's didactic approach had
imprinted all the details on the landlord's memory.

When that part of the narrative had concluded, Nessa Perks
paused long enough for Carole to ask, 'Had you ever met Burton
St Clair before last Tuesday?'

'Ah, that's the "FA" question. Predictable enough.'

'"FA question"?' Carole echoed.

'"Former Acquaintance". Much asked in Golden Age
mysteries – and no less in contemporary police enquiries. If
two apparently unrelated people turn out to have a shared
history, well, that information is obviously of great benefit to
any enquiry.'

The Professor was silent, as though the question had been
fully answered, so Carole ventured to ask, 'So, had you?'

'Had I what?'

'Had you ever met Burton St Clair before last Tuesday?'

'No. No, I had not.'

'And of the three possible scenarios you outlined—'

'The *only* three possible scenarios,' Nessa Perks insisted.

'Very well. Which one do you think applies in this case?'

'This is very definitely "MKH",' she pronounced.

'"Mistress Kills Husband"?'

'Indubitably.'

'What makes you so sure?'

'Carole, you take my word for it. That conclusion is the result of an entire career of research.'

'Right. So maybe you could spell out the details for me?'

'Of course. The most important factor in my deduction here is the comparative newness of Burton St Clair's marriage. He had been married to Persephone for less than six months. Now, from my exhaustive reading of Golden Age mysteries, I have extrapolated a set of statistics about the length of time that will elapse before a marriage becomes toxic. As a general rule, husbands and wives do not murder each other until well into their cohabitation. Except in the cases of contested wills or marriages undertaken for the sole purpose of inheritance, staples both of the "Sensation" novel of the late Victorian period, there is very little evidence of homicidal activity during the first six months after the wedding.'

'The honeymoon period?' Carole suggested.

'If you like,' said the Professor, in a manner that suggested only a non-academic would use such a frivolous expression. 'Intermarital resentment is something which tends to build up over a period of years rather than months.'

Thinking back to her own failed marriage to David, Carole could not but agree. 'Have you ever been married?' she asked suddenly. Nessa Perks seemed such a remote and shrink-wrapped personality; it was hard to imagine her having any normal bodily functions, let alone relationships – and certainly not sex.

'I did contract an incautious union during my sophomore year,' came the reply, 'which four years later, after college, developed into a marriage. It did not last.' And with that the subject was closed.

'If you could spell out a little more of your "MKH" theory?' asked Carole humbly.

'Of course. As I said, homicidal activity is very rare in the first six months of cohabitation, for which reason I would exclude Persephone St Clair from my primary list of suspects.'

'But Burton St Clair's current mistress would be in the frame?'

Professor Vanessa Perks shook her head firmly. 'No, it wouldn't be a current mistress.' Carole wondered what it must be like to go through life with such unshakable certainty that one was always right. 'No, for a man of Burton St Clair's age, a new marriage would be a completely new start. A *tabula rasa*.' Assuming, incorrectly, that Carole did not understand the Latin expression, she provided a gloss. 'A blank slate.'

'Yes, I do know—'

'So, embarking on a new marriage, Burton St Clair would have ended all other romantic entanglements.'

Not if he has the character Jude has described to me, thought Carole.

'As a suspect, we are looking therefore for a former mistress.'

'And her motivation?'

'In Golden Age mystery fiction, there are only five reasons to commit murder.' As she must have done in many lectures and seminars, she enumerated them on her fingers. 'Cover-Up, Revenge, Insanity, Money and Sex. Which fit rather neatly into the mnemonic: "CRIMS"—'

'Erm,' Carole interrupted, 'aren't there a few other possible motivations for murder? Surely there are also—?'

'No, there are just the five,' said the Professor in a voice that brooked no argument. 'Believe me, I have done a lot of research on the subject. Now, in this case, looking across the CRIMS spectrum, I would say we're definitely looking at "S". Sex. Burton St Clair had a complicated emotional route to finding his perfect partner in the form of Persephone. He had a lot of relationships . . .'

'He also had a former marriage.'

'Yes, I know that, Carole.' This was made to sound like a reprimand. 'I have obviously done a lot of research on him. And it seems that he was responsible for various infidelities during the period of his first marriage. So I would say definitely what we are looking at here is "RIADBSC" scenario.'

'"RIADBSC"?' came the feeble echo from Carole.

'"Revenge is a dish best served cold",' Nessa translated fluently. 'A very popular scenario with Golden Age mystery writers. An offence is allowed to rankle for a very long time, and finally, when the offendee can take no more pain and humiliation, his or her restraint snaps and the result is inevitably homicide.' Professor Vanessa Perks sat back and took a sip of Earl Grey, confident that she had produced an unanswerable thesis.

'Very well,' said Carole. 'Sorry if I'm being stupid, but could you tell me how that applies in the current case?'

'You're not being stupid,' said the Professor magnanimously, 'it's just that very few people's brains work at the rate that mine does. This was something which came apparent in high school, and since then it's just something I've had to live with.'

Carole was tempted to say, 'Bad luck,' but thought that might be seen as just another example of her lack of gravitas.

'In this case,' Nessa Perks condescended, 'the person we have to look for in our search for the murderer is the woman whose affair with Burton St Clair broke up his first marriage. That woman got a considerable charge out of seeing off his original wife Megan. It was very good for her self-esteem and she reckoned that, following the break-up, Burton St Clair was her property. She has continued to believe that ever since.'

Carole felt she had to intervene. 'Just a minute, we are talking about fifteen-odd years here.'

'Very common in cases of "RIADBSC",' said Nessa. 'The longer the perceived offence has had time to fester, the more violent the explosion when it is finally unleashed.'

'And why suddenly should all that violence be unleashed?'

'Well, obviously in this case, because of Burton St Clair's second marriage. His mistress has nursed the fantasy of his being exclusively hers for many years, put up with all kinds of lapses and infidelities, because finally she believes he will see reason and devote himself to her. No doubt he has also provided her with a plethora of reasons why the two of them cannot be married. But when he remarries someone else, that fantasy is no longer sustainable. The disillusionment is total. The long-term mistress, the woman who broke up his first marriage, realizes the only means she has to prevent her former paramour from the enjoyment of his new-found love is to kill him. So that is what she does.'

'Hm.' Carole let this sink in for a moment. Then she said, 'And can you put a name to this homicidal ex-mistress?'

'No,' came the frustrated reply. 'I suppose the police will have to sort that out.'

'They still haven't talked to you about the case?'

'No. Which is extremely lax of them. You'd have thought, having a homicide expert right on their doorstep, they would have made contact with me.'

'Perhaps,' Carole suggested gently, 'they are unaware that they have a homicide expert on their doorstep?'

'Maybe you're right,' the Professor conceded. 'Though I am internationally known and respected, that is probably more in academic than police circles. It would probably make sense for me to get in touch and put them out of their misery.'

'Might be a good idea, yes.'

Nessa Perks nodded to herself and then became aware of her hostess duties. 'Would you like some more tea?'

'Yes, please.'

'I'll make a fresh pot.'

While the Professor busied herself with her English tea ceremony, Carole reflected that communicating her theory to the police would not be very helpful to Jude's cause. The scenario Nessa had outlined was all too close to the one that the official enquiry seemed to be favouring.

Once they were both set up with more Earl Grey, Carole ventured to ask the homicide expert where, if she were investigating the murder, she would next direct her enquiries.

'Oh, I don't do hands-on investigation,' said the Professor. 'I'm a theorist, an armchair detective.'

'Of course. But who, connected to the case, would you talk to next?'

'The victim's second wife, Persephone St Clair.'

Which, Carole reflected, was the first sensible idea Professor Vanessa Perks had had all afternoon.

NINETEEN

Jude was getting sick of what felt to her like house arrest in Woodside Cottage, but at least Zosia had offered her a subject for investigation to which Detective Inspector Rollins could offer no objection. The disappearance of Uncle Pawel could not possibly have anything to do with the murder of Burton St Clair. After the confusions of the last few days, it would do Jude's soul good to feel that she was helping one of her fellow creatures.

And she was not without ideas for ways of tracking down the old reprobate.

Though Zosia had not voiced the anxiety, it had been clear she was worried that her uncle might be dead. She knew how vulnerable he could be when drunk, and had mentioned the anti-immigrant feeling which seemed to be growing along the South Coast. Her fears had probably also been exacerbated by constant talk in the Crown & Anchor about the murder at the library.

But Jude was not ready to be so pessimistic. There were many other explanations apart from death for the disappearance of someone in Uncle Pawel's condition. And through her work as a healer, there were plenty of avenues Jude could explore.

But before she could translate her intentions into action, the phone in Woodside Cottage rang. Part of her was relieved to hear the voice of Oliver Parsons.

'Just calling to bring you up to date on the official investigation into Burton St Clair's death,' he said languidly.

'I thought I told you I'd been warned off showing any interest in that subject.'

'Yes, you did. But I don't see why that stops me from ringing and giving you updates.'

'I'm not so sure.'

'What do you mean?'

'I think it's quite possible that my phone's bugged.'

'Oh, Jude, now you're just being paranoid.'

'Am I?' She wished she felt as certain as Oliver sounded.

'Well, even if you are being bugged, I'm at liberty to call you when I think fit. I haven't been warned off the investigation, have I?'

'I don't know.'

'I can assure you I haven't. And I have the kind of personality for whom being warned off only makes me keener to do whatever I've been forbidden. Anyway, I wanted to tell you that I have recently been interviewed by the police.'

'Oh?'

'Yes, I've now had my one-to-one – one-to-two, I should more accurately say – with Detective Inspector Rollins and Detective Sergeant Knight. Presumably they're working through everyone who was in the audience on Tuesday night.'

His words gave Jude an absurd little flicker of encouragement. Maybe somebody who'd been at Fethering Library that evening would be able to produce some evidence that would point to the real murderer of Burton St Clair, and that might let her off the hook.

Oliver Parsons' next words nurtured that hope. 'Anyway, in the course of interrogating me, Rollins and Knight did let slip something I found of interest.'

'Oh?'

'I'd made it clear to them that I was up to speed with the background to the case.'

'I doubt if they were very pleased to hear that.'

'I got the impression they'd heard something similar from everyone they'd interviewed. As you know, everyone in Fethering has their own views about the murder.'

'Yes.'

'So I didn't hold back on my own.'

'I'm sure you didn't.'

'And I mentioned what seems to be common knowledge in the village . . .' He speeded up as he went through the familiar rigmarole. '. . . that Burton St Clair is believed to have been poisoned by some walnut product infiltrated into the red wine bottle, which subsequently got broken.' He slowed down again. 'And that led to an interesting exchange between the two coppers.' He paused for effect.

'Oh, come on, Oliver, don't keep me in suspense!'

'Well, Detective Inspector Rollins then said, "That's just speculation. We have no proof that's how the murder happened." And her sidekick chipped in, "In fact, we now have forensic proof that that *isn't* how it happened." Well, she nearly bit his head off when he said that. Clearly, he was giving away more information than she thought appropriate. I had the feeling there was already a bit of friction between them.'

'Oh yes, there certainly was.' Jude was excited now. 'So you got the impression that forensic examination of the broken wine bottle had revealed no traces of walnut extract?'

'That is exactly the impression I got,' said Oliver.

'That's marvellous!'

'I thought you'd be pleased to hear it.'

'I am – ecstatic. Because if there was no trace of walnut in the bottle, then I couldn't have put it there!'

'Precisely. So, if it was the walnut allergy that killed Burton St Clair, then the offending nut extract must have been fed to him some other way.'

'Yes.'

'You don't have any idea what that other way might have been . . . do you, Jude?'

She felt really energized by Oliver's phone call. It offered the first hint of solid proof that she had no connection with Burton St Clair's murder. Her first instinct was to ring Detective Inspector Rollins immediately and challenge her adversary with the new information.

But it was an instinct she curbed. She'd no wish to antagonize the police any more than she had already. Wait till they came back to her, that was the way to play it. Leave the Fethering Library investigation to Carole for the time being. And concentrate on the case where her involvement wouldn't upset anyone – the disappearance of Zosia's Uncle Pawel.

There have always been many secrets hidden behind the placid exteriors of English country villages. Long before Agatha Christie popularized the crimes of the locations, there had been an undertow of drunkenness, debauchery, domestic violence and murder. And such antisocial tendencies had not diminished in the twenty-first century, even in a place as outwardly genteel as Fethering.

Through her work as a healer, Jude encountered much evidence of the darker side of village life. It was rarely that clients came to Woodside Cottage with ailments that were purely physical. (Indeed, Jude doubted whether any human ailments were *purely* physical.) The tension in a woman's back could arise from her husband's bullying. A schoolgirl's anorexia could be triggered by her parents' divorce. Depression could be exacerbated by a drug or alcohol problem. Jude always had to find the root cause of her client's suffering before she could begin the process of healing.

And it might have surprised an outsider to find out how many nice middle-class façades in Fethering masked serious problems with drugs and alcohol. Though Jude's ministrations in these cases could make some initial headway, often to achieve long-term benefits the sufferer would need to be referred for specialist treatment. As a result, Jude had contacts in all of the local organizations which dealt with the problems of substance abuse and alcohol dependency.

Her first call was to Karla. Of mountainous proportions and multiple tattoos, this woman had survived two decades of using drugs and abusing booze, with all the concomitant baggage of domestic violence, unwanted pregnancies, children being taken into care and prison sentences. Her shattered life turned around by courses run by a local charity, Karla had then decided to devote her remaining years to helping others out of the hell from which she had emerged. Nothing could shock her, she was unflappable, and every day for her was still a battle against the temptations offered by her former chemical supports.

That Sunday afternoon, Jude could tell as soon as Karla spoke that something had upset her. 'What's happened?'

'Just a boy, someone I'd been working with, topped himself.'

'I'm sorry.'

'Yes. Really thought we were getting somewhere with him. He'd come to a lot of meetings, been clean for nearly three months. Then fell in with some of his old crowd, they offered him some stuff. He jumped off the top of a car park in Worthing.'

'It must be hard for you.'

'He was getting somewhere and . . .' A deep, throaty sigh sounded from the other end of the line. 'Anyway, what can I do, Jude? Someone else needs referring?'

'No, it's not that this time. I'm trying to track down a guy who's in with a bunch of drinkers.'

'Living on the street?'

'Well, he has got somewhere to live, but I gather he spends a lot of time on the streets drinking.'

'Where?'

'Fethering, Littlehampton, gone as far as Brighton sometimes, I gather.'

'What's your contact with him?'

'I know his niece, works in our local pub.'

'Is that the old Crown & Anchor?'

'Yes. You know it?'

'Know it, yes. Never been in it. A bit upmarket for me back in my drinking days. Anyway, didn't do pubs when I was really drinking. Been barred from most of them in Littlehampton, apart from anything else. I was more cans of supermarket lager in a seafront shelter.'

'This bloke who's disappeared did that too.'

'Right, let's get a few basics. What's his name?'

'Pawel.'

'Oh?'

'He's Polish.'

'Right. There are a few of them around. Surname?'

'Haven't got one for him. I'll find out from his niece.'

'It's not that important. Most of them just use first names.'

'His niece, who's called Zosia, is putting him up in her flat, but she hasn't seen him since last Tuesday.'

'I'll ask around and get back to you,' said Karla.

Which was very comforting to hear. The investigation into Uncle Pawel's disappearance could not have been in better hands.

TWENTY

Jude woke on the Monday morning in a totally different frame of mind. The news from Oliver Parsons about the negative forensic tests on the wine bottle from the library staff room, though not yet officially confirmed, had brought back her old *joie de vivre*. She berated herself for the unaccustomed gloom into which she had sunk over the previous few days.

Now she no longer felt she had to find Burton St Clair's murderer to save her own skin. But that had not diminished her interest in the case. If anything, it had increased her enthusiasm for solving it.

After breakfast, she went on to her little-used Facebook account and made the contact she wanted to. Then she bounced ebulliently round to High Tor.

Even before Carole had produced coffee, Jude announced, 'I'm back on the case. I'm no longer going to be bossed around by the likes of Detective Inspector Rollins.'

'That's very good news, but can you tell me what's made you change your mind?'

Quickly, Jude brought her neighbour up to speed with what she'd heard from Oliver Parsons.

'Excellent,' said Carole, though an unworthy part of herself felt a little put out. She had been pleased with the way the investigation had been proceeding with her in sole charge. The idea of having Jude back at full throttle caused a momentary pang. From a child, Carole Seddon had never been that good at sharing.

'Anyway,' she went on, 'I have decided that, for the next stage of our investigation, we need to contact—'

'Persephone St Clair!'

Carole was miffed by the interruption, because that was exactly what she had been about to say. And her nose wasn't immediately set back in joint by Jude going on, 'What's more, I've just this morning made contact with her.'

'How? Have you got their home number?'

'No, I did it through Facebook.' Carole's sour expression said everything about her views of social media. 'And what's more, she's agreed that we can go over to Barnes to talk to her this morning!'

From Carole's point of view, in that sentence the 'we' was the only word that was welcome. She had had her own plans as to how she was going to contact Persephone St Clair, and she didn't like having them pre-empted. Still, she worked hard not to let her annoyance show, as Jude rushed back to Woodside Cottage to fetch a warm coat.

As Carole closed the front door of High Tor, Gulliver looked up wistfully from his station by the Aga. It was as if he could tell when his owner was busy on a case.

Having not had long to adjust to the idea of being a wife, Persephone St Clair seemed to have acclimatized very quickly to being a widow. There was a dramatic quality to the way she carried herself, as though preparing to deliver a great speech of bereavement.

She was very pretty in a slightly Kensington way. Round the thirty mark, so a good twenty years younger than Burton. Nor had he just gone for a younger model of Megan. While his first wife had been dark and petite, Persephone was blonde and willowy. She had the kind of upper-crust looks which, Carole recalled, used to feature on the inside pages of *Country Life*.

The interior of the house in Barnes might have come from the pages of a more contemporary lifestyle magazine. Money from the royalties and international sales of *Stray Leaves in Autumn* had been poured unstintingly into the pockets of interior architects and designers. There was no feeling of an individual stamp on anything. Al Sinclair, Jude recalled, like many writers, had been almost completely unaware of his surroundings, so any personal touches must have come from his new wife. Looking around the house, Jude reckoned that Persephone, thrilled with the unlimited budget she'd been given, had just opted for the most expensive of everything.

This was reflected in the brand-new BMW sports model parked outside the house. His and Hers Beamers.

The kitchen was further evidence of conspicuous consumption. It was an archipelago of islands, of marble, granite, glass and brushed steel. Every appliance was state-of-the-art. Its antiseptic cleanliness made even the kitchen at High Tor look welcoming.

Having taken their coffee orders and set the state-of-the-art machine in motion, Persephone volunteered to Carole and Jude that she had worked in the publicity department of the firm which published *Stray Leaves in Autumn*. 'Still working there. Well, haven't been in there the last week, obviously. Work under my maiden name. Persephone Sackwright-Newbury.' As this would suggest, her voice combined the tinkle of cut glass with the crackle of fifty-pound notes. 'The idea was that I would continue working until . . .' Her dark blue eyes glazed with tears.

They were meant to complete the unfinished sentence in their minds. Until she became pregnant, they both surmised. They were also meant to complete the implication, that it now would be Persephone's tragedy never to carry Burton's child. Jude, not a habitual cynic, suspected that, just as he had with Megan, the author would once again have put off permanently the creation of any rival to his pre-eminence in his own household.

Persephone did not seem to need any prompts to continue her heartbreaking narrative. 'We got to know each other when I was looking after Burton on the publicity tour for the hardback of *Stray Leaves*. We just clicked.'

In some hotel in Manchester, Jude surmised. Or maybe Glasgow, or Leeds. Two people thrown together by work – a fifty-something author of waning charms and wandering hands, a beautiful younger woman impressed by his success and watching her twenties drift away. A few drinks at a talk and book signing, more drinks in the hotel bar, then the minibar in one or other of their rooms – it was not difficult to fill in the details of how the affair started. The only surprise, really, was that it had gone the distance into marriage.

'Presumably,' said Carole, feeling it was about time they got down to the business of investigation, 'the police have talked to you about your husband's death?'

'Oh yes,' Persephone replied in tragic mode. 'It was from

them that I first heard about it. I hadn't worried about Burton not coming back on Tuesday night. He'd left it open whether he'd come home or stay in a hotel.' (Softening his new wife up for when he embarked on future infidelities, thought Jude cynically.) 'But then on Wednesday morning . . . The knock on the door that you've heard so often on television dramas, but which you never thought would be for you. It was terrible.'

'It must have been,' Carole agreed briskly.

'Just so appalling . . . the idea that Burton will never write another book like *Stray Leaves*.'

Jude could think of a lot of little old ladies in Fethering who would agree with that sentiment. She thought she herself would probably manage to survive the tragedy. But she felt one of them ought to show a little sympathy for the girl and, not expecting it to come from Carole, said, 'It must be terrible for you, Persephone, to be widowed so early into your married life.'

'It is,' the girl acknowledged with a devout lowering of her head. 'I will never get over it. I will never love again.'

Entirely appropriate sentiments for a woman not a week widowed, but somehow Jude suspected that Persephone was young enough to bounce back. She'd got the impression that one of the attractions of marriage had been the prospect of starting a family, and felt sure there were plenty of young men out there who'd be more than happy to have such a beautiful mother for their children. Jude also wondered whether Persephone's parents might not be happier with a new son-in-law nearer their daughter's age than their own. She did not think the girl's future would be wholly grim.

Carole was still keen to get on with the business of detection. 'Apart from the police's notifying you of your husband's death, they have presumably also interviewed you about how it happened?'

'Oh yes. Of course, I was in a terrible state of shock, but I tried to answer their questions as well as I could.'

And you enjoyed every minute of it, thought Jude. She was slightly surprised that the girl brought out such deep cynicism in her. Maybe it reflected the ambivalence she'd always felt towards Burton himself. She had a feeling that, in his marriage to Persephone, shallow had called to shallow.

'Presumably,' Carole persisted, 'you were told that your husband died from anaphylactic shock after ingesting something with walnut in it?'

'They told me that, yes.'

'And you were aware of his walnut allergy?'

'Of course. It was heavily marked up on his notes. When we were touring the country promoting *Stray Leaves*, I had to check the menu for literary lunches, that kind of thing. And also ensure that he never went anywhere without his EpiPen.'

'He did have it with him when he left here on Tuesday for Fethering?'

'Oh, certainly.'

'Where would he carry it?' asked Jude. 'In his jacket pocket?'

'Most of the time. If he was driving, he'd put it in the glove compartment of the car.'

'So it's possible that's where he put it on Tuesday?'

'Yes. He definitely did. The police told me so. That's where they found it. Though why he couldn't get to it in time when he felt the anaphylactic shock coming on, I'll never know . . .' Once again, she dissolved into self-regarding tears.

'Where did Burton usually carry his car keys?' asked Carole suddenly. 'In his trouser pocket?'

'No. He always said he didn't like to spoil the line of his trousers by having more than a handkerchief in the pockets.' Persephone let out a tragic little chuckle. 'I'm afraid even someone like Burton did have his little vanities.' They were the main component of his personality, thought Jude, as the widow went on, 'He always put his car keys in his jacket pocket. And his wallet. And his small change, come to that.'

Carole and Jude exchanged looks. They were both thinking the same thing: that the author's leather jacket had been left in the Fethering Library staff room, from where his car keys could have been extracted by anyone who wanted to get into his 'Beamer'.

The mention of the car's glove compartment started a new thought in Jude's mind. 'Back when I spent time with Al . . . Burton,' she began tentatively, 'he used to drink quite a lot.'

Persephone chuckled. 'Occupational hazard for writers. For publishers too, come to that. Friend of mine once described publishing as "an industry floated on a sea of alcohol". Certainly, Burton and I always used to bond over a bottle of wine . . . or two.' The recollection brought a catch to her throat. With an effort, she continued, 'Anyway, Burton concentrated so ferociously when he was writing, that when he stopped he always needed what he called "a couple of stiff ones", to bring him back into the real world.'

'Would you have said he had a drink problem?' asked Carole, who didn't know where Jude's enquiry was leading.

'Oh, good heavens, no, Burton could hold his drink. He never appeared drunk. I've never seen him drunk. He's always – that is, he always *was* – very articulate when he's – when he was – drinking. Had the odd hangover, of course, went with the territory, but that never stopped him from being behind his keyboard, writing, at nine o'clock in the morning. He was like Hemingway, in that respect.'

And saw himself as like Hemingway in many other respects. Not just the great drinker, but the great adventurer, the great womanizer, the great innovating writer. None of which he was, thought Jude uncharitably. Though that was not what she said. 'Back when I saw a lot of Burton . . .' she began.

'Back when he was with his first wife?'

'Yes.'

'That bitch Megan.'

'She was a friend of mine,' said Jude, scrupulously fair in such matters. 'She was never a bitch to me, not back then, anyway. But I'm sure you've heard a different version of her from Burton. Ex-partners are not always each other's best character witnesses.'

'Huh. Well, from everything I've heard, Burton was well out of that marriage.'

'Maybe.'

'Megan totally ignored him. All she thought about was her career.' Jude did not make any further comment. 'And she didn't like sex, that's for sure. Burton had to beg and plead to get even a kiss from her. From everything he said about her, it was pretty clear that she was frigid.'

Still, Jude bit her tongue, as she listened to the litany of complaint that so many men over the ages have levelled at their former partners. But she wasn't prepared for what Persephone said next.

'It was Megan's frigidity that drove Burton into your arms, Jude.'

Oh God, that was completely typical. Burton had taken over Megan's lie about their affair and made it his own. Perhaps, with the passage of the years, he had convinced himself of its truth just as much as his ex-wife had. Or, more likely, he had used the story to provide some kind of justification for the break-up of his first marriage. Either way, he had convinced Persephone that the relationship had happened.

Jude looked across at Carole and saw from the beadiness in her eye that she'd get no support from that quarter. Carole's wild fantasies about her neighbour's sex life had just received further confirmation.

The record would have to be set straight at some point, but right now Jude had more important priorities. 'Back when I saw a lot of Burton,' she repeated, 'it wasn't just the wine that he drank. He also got through a great deal of whisky. In fact, he always used to carry around a hipflask full of the stuff.'

'Oh, yes, he still did that,' said Persephone St Clair. 'He had this horrible old pewter thing. I bought him a new silver one as a wedding present. But whenever Burton went off to a speaking gig, he always had the hipflask in the glove compartment of his car.'

In the immaculate Renault on the way back to Fethering, Jude didn't say how exultant she felt, but Carole could sense the euphoria bubbling up from the passenger seat. It was only now the threat had been lifted, that Jude realized just how much stress the suspicions of the last week had put on her. As soon as the car stopped outside Woodside Cottage, she rushed inside to make an essential phone call.

Detective Inspector Rollins answered at the first ring.

'It's Jude.'

'Ah, yes. I was expecting you to call. I hope you had a pleasant visit to Persephone St Clair.'

A few hours earlier those words would have been deeply unsettling, but now nothing could cast Jude down. 'I did, thank you very much,' she replied. 'And I suggest you can probably lift the surveillance on me now.'

A harsh laugh echoed down the line. 'If you think we can afford police resources to keep someone like you under surveillance, then you flatter yourself.'

'Then how did you know?'

'Mrs St Clair rang to tell us you were going.'

'Oh. And did she also tell you about the hipflask of whisky that her husband habitually carried with him?'

'She did, but we'd already known about that for a long time. As have you.'

'What do you mean by that?'

'Megan Sinclair said you spoke to her about the hipflask when you met last week.'

'Well, she reminded me about it.'

'She said you brought the subject up.'

'That's just not true!'

The Inspector's silence made Jude realize just how guilty her protestations made her sound. She took a deep breath to regain control and said, 'Presumably you haven't found the hipflask?'

'No.'

'Well, if no trace of walnut was found on the pieces of the broken wine bottle . . .' Jude was encouraged that the Inspector did not even question that assertion, '. . . then presumably you might be thinking that the substance might have been put into the hipflask instead?'

'Of course we have considered that possibility, Jude,' Rollins said testily.

'Anyway, whichever way you look at the situation, it means I'm no longer on your list of suspects, doesn't it?'

'Why not?'

'Well, for heaven's sake!' Jude contained her anger, and went on calmly, 'Whereas I might, by some stretch of the imagination, have had the opportunity to infiltrate walnut oil into the open bottle of wine in the library staff room, how am I supposed to have got it into a hipflask in the glove compartment of Burton St Clair's car? Surely it's more likely that the hipflask was sabotaged at an earlier time, possibly even before he arrived in Fethering?'

'Jude, you are the only person known to have got into Burton St Clair's car that evening.'

'Yes, but I got into it when he was already in there! Are you suggesting that I sat in the passenger seat, with Burton watching, calmly removed his hipflask from the glove compartment, decanted some *huile de noix* and made him drink it, while all the time he was trying to grope me?'

'I am not suggesting that, no.'

'Thank God for small mercies.'

'On the other hand, I am saying that Burton St Clair's leather jacket, in which he carried his car keys, was left unattended in the library staff room. So it would in theory have been possible for someone—'

'Why not say *me*?'

'I said "someone", Jude . . . in the confusion of the evening, to have entered his car and poisoned the hipflask.'

'It sounds pretty unlikely.'

'In our enquiries the "unlikely" is something we can never rule out.'

'Huh.'

'So, if "someone" had done that, and the same "someone" had gone into his car later and encouraged him to take a swig from the hipflask, then—'

'Look, can you cut the "someone"? Why not name me? You've already said I'm the only person who got into his car that evening.'

'I said you were the only person *known* to have got into his car that evening.'

'So, say I did it, where's your evidence? Where's the hipflask, come to that? If Detective Sergeant Knight would like to conduct another search of Woodside Cottage, he's welcome to do it any time he likes. Send him round now, if you like!'

'That won't be necessary at this stage, thank you, Jude. Besides, I very much doubt that we would find anything.'

'Oh?'

'I don't need to tell you that Fethering is by the seaside. I would have thought anyone walking from the library along the front to the centre of the village with an incriminating hipflask in their pocket would have taken advantage of the facilities provided.'

'Chucked it in the sea, you mean?'

'That's exactly what I mean. We'd be very unlikely to find it there.'

'So, what you are saying basically, Detective Inspector Rollins, is that I am still on your list of suspects?'

'Yes, and I'm afraid you will remain there until we find some actual proof of your innocence.'

'I see,' said Jude.

But her mood was no longer feeble and paranoid. Now she was just furiously angry.

TWENTY-ONE

I feel better,' said Jude, 'now I'm sharing what I know about the case with you.'

Carole tried not to show how much these words meant to her as she mumbled some platitude about two heads being better than one. They were in front of the open fire in the sitting room of Woodside Cottage. It was early for Jude to have opened a bottle of Sauvignon Blanc, but Carole had only raised a token objection.

'Anyway, the important thing,' she went on, 'is where we take our investigation on from here.'

'Since, according to Rollins, I had the opportunity to filch Burton's car keys from his leather jacket and put walnut oil into his hipflask, maybe we should be asking ourselves who else had that opportunity.'

'You know the list of suspects better than I do. Who've we got?'

'OK. The two members of the library staff, Di Thompson and Vix Winter. Then there's your friend Nessa Perks.'

Carole wrinkled her nose. 'I'd hardly call her my friend.'

'You know who I mean, anyway. Then there's Oliver Parsons . . .'

'*Your* friend.'

'Maybe,' Jude quickly dismissed the thought. 'And there's shelf-stacker and science-fiction writer *manqué*, Steve Chasen.'

'He's the one who verbally attacked Burton St Clair?'

'Yes.'

'Which is suspicious behaviour by any standards.'

'Mm. I was just thinking – there's a connection between Oliver and Steve that might be worth following up.'

'Oh?'

'They were both members of a Writers' Group that used to run at Fethering Library.'

'Ah well, there's another connection there.'

'Oh?'

'The woman you describe as *my* friend. Nessa Perks. She was involved in a few sessions with that set-up.' In response to Jude's look of puzzlement, Carole explained, 'I heard that from Di Thompson when I talked to her on Saturday.'

'That's interesting. Might be worth talking further to her, find out a bit more about the group.'

'Well, you could—'

Carole was interrupted by the phone ringing.

Jude answered it. 'Ah, Karla, thanks for getting back to me.'

She knew Carole was disappointed not to be included in the visit, but it wouldn't have been right for her to come. Though it didn't actually involve any of Jude's clients, she felt any dealings she had with Karla had to be confidential.

She had not been surprised when told to bring a bottle of vodka. Though Karla's long-term aim was to cure people, she knew that on occasions their addictions had to be fed. And that was certainly the case when information was required. There was a going rate for everything.

The rendezvous was between two beach huts on the seashore at Littlehampton. In daylight – and certainly in the summer tourist season – a drunkard would have been moved on from there, but on a dark late Monday afternoon in January, nobody was around to care.

Jude had got a cab and met Karla on the promenade that ran along the landward side of the rows of beach huts. She looked huge and more shapeless than ever, shrouded in a tent-like anorak with a fur-trimmed hood. 'His name's Lennie,' she said. 'He knows Pawel.'

Jude was aware of the smell before she saw the man. Urine, sweat and something else more noxious than either. Maybe the beach huts provided a degree of protection from the bitter wind that scoured the shingle, but it was still a miserable place to be. She didn't like to think where Lennie might be spending the night.

He was only an outline in the fading light, a dark coat tied round with a belt from a lighter garment. A woollen hat was pulled down over greasy hair. His glazed eyes were unfocused. His whole body trembled.

'Lennie,' said Karla, 'this is Jude, the woman I told you about.'

'And did she bring what you promised?' he asked.

His voice was a shock to Jude. Through the slurring and the hiss of missing teeth, it was educated, even public school educated.

'Yes,' said Karla.

'Hello, Lennie,' said Jude, and she handed across the vodka bottle.

He unscrewed it with a practised flick, and swigged down perhaps a quarter of the contents.

The effect was instantaneous. The trembling of his body ceased, and when he looked at her he seemed to take in her presence. 'Thank you,' he said. 'There was something you wanted to ask me about, I believe.'

'A Polish man called Pawel?'

'Ah, yes, of course.'

'You do know him?'

'Yes. We have drunk together.' He made it sound as if they had shared the occasional vintage bottle in a London gentleman's club.

'And talked together?'

'A little. He does not have much English.'

'When did you last see him?'

'Ah.' Lennie looked at her regretfully. 'I am not very good about time.'

'Recently?' He shrugged. 'In the last week?' He spread his hands wide in a gesture of helplessness.

'Come on, Lennie,' said Karla gently. 'Try to remember.'

'I am trying, but . . . nothing comes.'

'Can you remember,' asked Jude, 'not when you last saw him, but what happened when you last saw him?'

Lennie gave the question due consideration, but then slowly shook his head.

'*Where* you last saw him?'

'Who are we talking about?'

'Pawel.'

'Oh yes, Pawel.' His brow wrinkled with the effort of memory. 'Pawel? No, I didn't see Pawel here in Littlehampton.'

'Where then?'

'Is it in . . .?' But a look froze the words on Karla's lips. Jude did not want ideas to be planted in Lennie's mind. She waited for him to come up with the recollection himself.

After a long silence, she was rewarded. 'In Fethering,' he said slowly. 'I saw Pawel in Fethering.'

'Whereabouts in Fethering?'

'In the shelter by the beach.'

'When did you last see him there?'

But Jude's question was too insistent for him. He shook his head slowly and, as his eyes once again glazed over, he put the bottle to his lips and took another long pull of vodka.

There was another long silence. Then he spoke again. 'Last time I saw Pawel, he wanted some of my drink. I let him have a little. Not much. I needed it. He didn't have drink of his own.'

'Ah,' said Jude, not sure whether prompting him further was going to help.

'He didn't have drink of his own, but he had something he wanted to sell to buy drink.'

'What was that?' she asked breathlessly.

'Silver,' he said.

'Money?'

'No, made of silver. He said he knew someone who would buy it from him. A Polish person he knew. Some funny name; they all have funny names. Milo, perhaps . . .?'

'Lennie,' Jude repeated, 'what was it? What was the thing Pawel was going to sell?'

'A . . . what's it called? For drink.' He searched the fuddled recesses of his memory, and finally the word came to him. 'A hipflask.'

TWENTY-TWO

W hat's his story? I mean, that is, if you can tell me without breaching client confidentiality.'

Karla had offered to drive Jude back to Fethering in her battered Nissan Micra. They had left Lennie between the beach huts.

'No worries about that,' she replied. 'Lennie worked in advertising. Respectable job, mortgage, married. Probably drank too much, but in a nice middle-class way. Then his wife died, I don't know, five years ago perhaps. That's when he really started hitting the bottle. Soon wasn't turning up for work, lost his job. Couldn't pay the mortgage, the house was repossessed. Within a year, he was on the streets.'

'Was it responsible, giving him the bottle of vodka?'

Karla's massive shoulders shrugged. 'Stopped him from thieving to get some. And if you wanted the information . . .'

'Yes.'

'I've registered him on any number of alcohol-dependency courses. He goes to a couple of sessions, then gives up. The trouble is with all those programmes – AA, the lot – the individual has to have the will to give up the booze. Lennie hasn't got the will. He doesn't want to change. So, I give him what support I can, get him to a doctor if he's actually ill, sort out accommodation, but he never stays anywhere long.'

'He's got a death wish?'

Karla nodded grimly. 'Since his wife died, he doesn't want to live.'

'So there's nothing you can do about him?'

'I can keep trying.' But Karla didn't sound hopeful.

'And then one day he'll just be found on the street, dead?'

'Yes. There are some cases like that.'

Jude agreed. She'd had clients who were the same, people she just couldn't help. Not many, but she remembered them all very clearly, remembered them as failures on her part. Any kind of healing must have some input from the person being healed.

There was silence in the car until they reached Woodside Cottage.

She was pleased later that evening to have a call from Oliver Parsons. Particularly pleased because rather than going straight to the subject of the murder, he first chatted inconsequentially about the weather and the government's latest idiocy. It revived in Jude the thought that he might be interested in her as more than a fellow investigator.

But of course, in time he did get round to Burton St Clair's death. 'Just wondered if you'd heard anything new?' he asked, characteristically casual. 'Are you still the Number One Suspect?'

'Well, I thought for a moment I was off the hook.' And she quickly brought him up to speed with the lack of evidence on the wine bottle fragments and the new interest in Burton's hipflask.

'Ah, that's a turn-up,' Oliver commented slowly.

'So, the police are now looking for people who knew about his habit of taking a hipflask wherever he went. Which unfortunately doesn't get me out of the picture.'

'Oh?'

'Megan says I brought up the subject when we met for lunch on Thursday. Which isn't true. She brought it into the conversation. But I can't deny it was mentioned.'

'Megan seems to have got it in for you, doesn't she, Jude? Insisting you had an affair with Burton, an affair which broke up her marriage. Now insisting you mentioned the hipflask. Any idea why she's so violently anti you?'

'I just think she's mentally unbalanced.'

'Hmm.'

'Why, what are you thinking?'

'Well, Jude, if this were one of those Golden Age crime novels I used to spend a lot of time reading . . .'

'Yes?'

'Megan would be focusing suspicion on you to divert it away from herself.'

'But she couldn't have had anything to do with Burton's death. As we've established, on the relevant evening she was staying with her friend in Scarborough.'

'Yes, but if this were a Golden Age crime novel, she would have masterminded the murder and actually got someone else to do the poisoning.'

'Like who?'

'My suspicions keep coming back to Steve Chasen.'

'Why particularly?'

'Ever since I first met him, at the Fethering Library Writers' Group, I had the feeling I'd seen him before somewhere. And it's only recently I've worked it out.'

'You had met him before?'

'Not met, no. Seen.'

'I'm not with you?'

'Friend of mine from way back, guy called Rodge, was also a television director. Used to work on BBC arts programmes – back when the BBC *did* arts programmes. And there was one he did about the Wordway Trust.'

'The what?'

'The Wordway Trust. It's an organization that runs week-long residential courses for aspiring writers.'

'Oh.'

'They're tutored by professionals. There are a lot of charlatans out in the creative writing course business, but the Wordway Trust ones have quite a good reputation. Anyway, I was talking to Rodge a couple of days ago and he mentioned this film he'd made at a place called Blester Combe in Wiltshire – gosh, got to be fifteen years ago, probably more – and I realized that's where I recognized Steve Chasen from.'

'He was tutoring the course?'

'No, no, the tutors are all published authors. Steve was on the course as a participant.'

'An aspiring writer?'

'Exactly. Which is what, I'm sure he'd be very sorry to admit, he still is.'

'OK, so that's where you'd seen him before, but why is this relevant to the investigation?'

'It's relevant, Jude, because another aspiring writer on the same course – and Rodge just confirmed this to me – was called Al Sinclair.'

Di Thompson agreed to see Jude the following morning, the Tuesday. 'Come at nine. I'll be there, though we don't open till ten. Used to be nine to seven every day, but the hours have been cut back. And I'm sure they'll soon be cut back further. Money, as ever.'

Jude asked if Carole wanted to come along with her to the library, but got a frosty response. Her neighbour said she'd already spoken to Di, the implication being that fault was being found with the way she'd conducted the bit of the investigation she'd done on her own. Jude also suspected she acted that way because the impetus for the next stage of their enquiry had come from Oliver Parsons. Carole could be so Carole at times.

Being back at Fethering Library gave Jude both a literal and a metaphorical *frisson*. The weather seemed colder than ever, one of those cloud-compressed days when it would never be properly light and when the wind would continue to scythe its relentless way up from the beach. She could not help herself from wondering, a little guiltily, where Lennie had spent the night.

And being back at the library for the first time since she'd stormed away from Burton's car the previous week brought a chill to her soul as well.

When Di opened the door for her, it was almost as cold inside as out. 'Central heating takes quite a while to heat up,' the librarian explained. 'One of the other things in this place that should have been replaced long ago.' She had kept on her outside coat. Jude did the same.

'I'm afraid you'll just have to follow me around,' said Di. As she had when Carole talked to her, she was working with a trolley of books, but on this occasion she was wheeling it round the stacks, replacing returned books in their proper places.

'Can I help?' asked Jude.

'Probably simpler if I do it. I know where everything goes.'

Jude was surprised that someone of Di Thompson's status was doing such a seemingly menial task. 'I suppose all of your staff have to do a bit of everything . . .?' she ventured.

'"All my staff"?' she echoed ironically. 'That doesn't amount to very many, I'm afraid. A bunch of part-timers, only one permanent, apart from me.'

'Was that the girl who was helping last week? Is she the full-time one?'

'Yes, Vix . . . though her definition of full-time and my own are rather at variance.'

'My neighbour Carole Seddon talked to her during the week.'

'Yes, I know Carole. Comes when she's got her granddaughter with her. As do a lot of the ladies of Fethering. Sadly, they don't come that much on their own.'

'No.' Given the opening, Jude wanted to put the next bit tactfully. 'From what Carole said, Vix didn't seem to be that dedicated to her job.'

Fortunately, the librarian was more than ready to voice criticism of her junior. 'That's an understatement. When I started in the library service, the staff were a mixed bunch, like in any big organization, but at least they did like books, and knew about books. Many of us had relevant degrees. But with government cutbacks, local authorities can't afford to pay people with top librarian's qualifications. So they go for people with minimal training, call them library assistants, pay them very little, and hope they learn on the job. Which in some cases works very well – I've had colleagues with very bright and motivated library assistants, worked with a good few myself – but when someone like Vix Winter slips under the wire . . . well, it's very difficult to get rid of them.

'She's the original of what my father used to call "a jobsworth". For them, everything's more than their "job's worth". Didn't think there would be any in her generation, but Vix certainly qualifies. Kind of employee who's always talking about her "job description", and, whenever she's asked to do anything extra, saying she'll have to speak to her "line manager". It's a right pain. So, I mean, getting her to stay late for an event like Burton St Clair's talk on Tuesday – you'd think I'd asked her to assist in a major crime. In a place like a library, you must have staff who're prepared to go the extra mile, to help out occasionally without making a fuss. Well, I'm afraid you don't get that kind of co-operation from Miss Vix Winter.

'Which doesn't do wonders for the kind of service we can provide, and which is why I end up doing jobs that you'd have thought would be done by a junior.'

'You sound rather pessimistic about the future of libraries.'

'Difficult not to be. Particularly in a tiny branch like this. Fewer borrowings, fewer people using the facilities, already cutting qualified staff and opening hours. If this was a commercial business, it would have closed down years ago.'

'So why hasn't it closed down?'

Di shrugged at the hopelessness of the situation. 'Because people in this country like the idea of libraries. Part of the traditional fabric of our society – books, information, education readily available, free for everyone. Whenever they do market research on this kind of thing, it turns out that people *love* their libraries. God, if half the people who turn out for demonstrations against the closure of libraries actually went into their local branches a couple of times a week, the whole problem would be solved!

'But it's not just that. The online world has changed everything, and libraries have been slow to catch up. Yes, the Victorian, the Edwardian library was a fine institution. But whether that model works so well in the days of Google and Wikipedia is another matter. The trouble is, there are votes in having libraries. Politicians at the national and local level hate the idea of being seen to close them down. So they keep the places going, and gradually starve them of resources. And some finally close, and some stagger on as "community libraries", staffed by volunteers, and . . .' Her words trickled away to silence.

'Oh dear, I've really depressed myself now.' Di Thompson slammed a couple of books into their slots with excessive vigour. 'Sorry . . . Jude, was it?'

'Yes.'

'Well, Jude, I'm afraid you got me on my hobby-horse.'

'Don't apologize. I found it very interesting.'

'But it wasn't what you came in here to talk about?'

'No, it wasn't, actually.'

'You came in to talk about what happened to Burton St Clair here last Tuesday.' Responding to the puzzlement in Jude's face, Di said, 'That's still all anyone wants to talk about.'

'Well, it might be related to that.'

'Go on then.' The librarian looked at her watch. 'I can give you about five minutes. Then there's other stuff I've got to do before I open up.'

'Right, thanks. It's just . . . some of the people I was chatting to after the Burton St Clair talk mentioned a Creative Writers' Group you used to run here.'

'Oh yes. Well, it wasn't my plan to run it. I thought, when I had the idea, after a time it would become self-perpetuating, but it didn't work out that way. Another initiative that failed, another attempt to get the library used more, to get more people coming in and out.'

'How was it run?'

'I organized speakers, you know, to come to the first few sessions, to get things rolling, with the idea that the participants would then run it themselves. But nobody kind of stepped up to the plate, and I was doing so much other stuff I couldn't spare the time. Whole thing folded up within six months.'

'I heard about it from Oliver Parsons.'

'Oh yes?'

'He said Steve Chasen was a member too.'

Di nodded. 'Don't think they get on particularly well, those two.'

'The speakers you say you organized, who were they?'

'Local writers, people from other writers' groups, teachers from the sixth-form colleges and the university – anyone I could rope in, really.'

'Did Burton St Clair ever come to speak to them?'

'Good heavens, no. Last Tuesday was the first time he'd ever been to Fethering, so far as I know.'

'How did you get in touch with him? Had you got mutual friends?'

'It was through the publicity department of his publisher.'

'Ah.' Jude had been a little optimistic to think that line of

questioning would lead anywhere. 'Going off at a tangent, have
you heard of an organization called the Wordway Trust?'

'Yes. Set-up that runs residential writing courses?'

'That's it.'

'We've got some literature about them.' The librarian gestured
vaguely towards a flyer-covered table by the front doors.
'Supposed to be quite good, I think. Why, are you contemplating
taking up writing?'

'No way. I don't have that kind of creativity in me. Hated
writing essays at school. Reason I was asking about them is
that I heard Burton St Clair and Steve Chasen were once on
the same Wordway Trust course.'

'I didn't know that, but it sounds quite possible. Why, are
you thinking that Burton might have done something then to
antagonize Steve sufficiently for him to exact his revenge many
years later?'

The irony in her voice now verged on sarcasm, so Jude said,
'No, nothing like that. Well, look, I can't thank you enough,
Di, for your time, and for being so helpful. I'll pick up one of
the flyers for the Wordway Trust; might be some contact numbers
I could follow up on there.'

'Good morning!'

Both women looked up at the interruption. Di Thompson
showed surprise to see Eveline Ollerenshaw, dressed in a mangy
mink coat that predated anti-fur campaigns.

'I didn't think you were coming in today, Evvie,' said the
librarian. 'I thought we'd agreed that from now on you were
only going to do Wednesdays and Fridays.'

'Yes, but I know how busy you get. And I'm just next door.
I can see when the car park fills up and there are lots of customers.'

'There are no customers at this time in the morning,'
Di protested.

'No, but you know what I mean. It's no trouble for me to
pop in and lend a hand. Look, right now here's you putting
back the returned books. Someone in your position shouldn't
have to do that, Di. Particularly when I'm more than happy to
do it.'

'Yes, Evvie, but last time you did it, you may remember
there were a lot of books returned to the wrong sections.'

'Not many,' said the old lady defiantly. Then, after a silence, 'Are you telling me I should go home then?'

Remembering what she'd thought when she'd first met Eveline Ollerenshaw the week before, Jude realized that this was a big moment for Di Thompson. The librarian had been trying, tactfully, to ease out her well-meaning but inefficient volunteer. She had suggested, and thought they'd agreed, to reduce her number of days, but Evvie was now trying it on, testing the strength of her boss's resolution.

Di Thompson failed the test. 'Very well,' she said. 'I could use some help this morning. Just this morning, though.'

'All right. I'll just go and put my coat away.' And Eveline Ollerenshaw, fully aware of her triumph, scuttled away to the staff room.

Jude grinned ruefully, but made no comment. 'I'd better be on my way. But thanks so much for all your help, Di.'

'No problem.' Then, as Jude moved away, the librarian said, 'Oh, thinking about the Wordway Trust, there's another approach you could try.'

'Mm?'

'One of our regulars in the library, woman named Nemone Coote – quite a successful poet, I gather . . . Well, a published poet, which I think does mean successful these days. I know she's always coming in when she has a new collection out to check we've got it in stock. Might be worth getting in touch with her.'

'Oh?'

'Yes, she used to be in charge of one of the venues where the Wordway Trust courses were run.'

TWENTY-THREE

Before meeting Nemone Coote, Jude had done her homework by reading the Wordway Trust flyer from the library. When contacted by telephone, the woman had been only too ready to talk. Like Nessa Perks, she seemed disappointed that the police had not yet been in touch with her. She too thought they were neglecting the presence of an expert in their midst. Jude wondered whether the two women might know each other.

Nemone lived in a small village near Clincham, but was very happy to drive to meet up. 'Those of us who work from home will do anything to get out of the house, you know – particularly on those days when the ideas aren't flowing.' They agreed on the Crown & Anchor – yes, she knew the pub – at five o'clock for 'a glass and a chat.' Jude felt a momentary pang for not including her neighbour in the encounter, but after the sniffy way Carole had behaved that morning . . .

Nemone Coote was a bulky woman with short-cropped white hair. Despite the weather, she wore pink Croc clogs, shin-length jeans and a sleeveless, almost Hawaiian shirt over her flat chest. Had Central Casting been looking for someone to play a butch lesbian, she would have walked it. Ordering a pint of Guinness did nothing to dispel the image.

As she ordered the drinks from Ted Crisp at the bar, Jude thought of Zosia. She hadn't had the opportunity to tell the girl about her encounter with Lennie the night before. 'Zosia not around?'

'Doesn't work this shift,' said the landlord.

Of course. Zosia had said her day off was Tuesday. It was the previous one when she'd cooked *kopytka* for her Uncle Pawel. And that was the last time she'd seen him. So, if Zosia provided an alibi for him that evening, how had the hipflask come into his hands? A question Jude would have to follow up. But not at that moment. Nemone Coote was her first priority.

'I was a Centre Director at Blester Combe for nearly five years,' the poet announced.

'Blester Combe is the Wordway Trust place in Wiltshire?'

'That's right. They have three centres round the country. Big "houses in the country", rather than "country houses" – that would give very much the wrong impression. Nothing posh about them: old farmhouses, that kind of place, which have been converted by Wordway. Accommodating up to twenty

– you know, the centre staff, the tutors and the participants. The number of them on each course is capped at sixteen.'

'And courses run right through the year?'

'Pretty much. It was a job that suited me, you know, at that stage of my career. I'd just had my first collection published. *Divergent Parallels* – don't know if you've read it?'

'Sorry, no.'

'Published by Blue Gudgeon. Got very warm reviews. I was described as "a voice that rejects the old tropes of traditional poetry and brings in new tropes".'

'Oh. Well. Congratulations.'

'But obviously, I couldn't make a living from the poetry at that stage, so the Blester Combe job just suited me. Offered the chance of mixing with other writers, you know, the tutors, so perhaps learning more about my craft. And when I took it on, I thought it would give me time to get on with my own writing. That, sadly, proved not to be the case. Hardly wrote a word for five years. Pretty full-on job, being Centre Director.'

'What does it involve?'

'What doesn't it involve? Organizing the cleaning and bed-making on the changeover days, welcoming the new participants – in some cases, fetching them from the station. Supervising the cooking – they cook the evening meals themselves, you know. Then seeing the tutors are happy. Sorting out problems, which can range from facilitating wheelchair access to extricating the participants from each other's beds.' She chuckled heartily. 'And fielding endless complaints about everything from virtually everyone. Let me tell you, it's no picnic being a Wordway Trust Centre Director.'

'Ah.'

'In fact, I wrote about the experience – subtly disguised, of course, to avoid libel risks – in my second collection, *It's No Picnic*. Published by Intravenous Press. I don't suppose you . . .'

'I'm afraid not.'

'No.' Nemone Coote sadly shook her head, inured over many years to the blindness of a world which had yet to recognize her genius.

'I actually wanted to talk about Burton St Clair.'

'Ah, yes.' This sparked new enthusiasm in the woman. If her

own poetry was not going to bring her centre stage, having
information about a murder could be her next best claim to
fame.

'It's a long shot I know, Nemone, but Burton St Clair –
calling himself Al Sinclair back then – did once attend a
Wordway crime fiction course at Blester Combe. You weren't
by any chance there as Centre Director when he . . .?'

Nemone Coote's beaming smile told Jude the answer before
she needed to complete her question. 'Yes, I was. And I must
say it's always very encouraging when Blester Combe participants go on to success in the publishing world. You know, I
feel that I have in some way contributed to what's happened to
them.'

'Of course,' said Jude, uncertain what the nature of Nemone's
contribution might have been.

'It's a sort of vicarious nurturing, you know. Like being a
parent at one remove, an emotional situation that I embrace in
my poem, *Parent at One Remove*. From the collection, *And a
Partridge in a Parent*, published by the Black Willy imprint. I
don't know if you . . .' Jude shook her head. 'No. Anyway,
I recognized the talent in Al Sinclair – it just seemed to be
bursting out of him. So much talent, so much energy . . .
Irrepressible he was. I think that's why he came on to all of
the women on the course – just pure animal energy.'

'Ah.'

'He came on to me too, you know.'

'Did he?'

'Yes. End of a long evening, we were stacking the dishwasher,
and he put his hand on my breast. I had to tell him it wasn't
appropriate.'

'Right.'

'You know, with my position of being Centre Director.'

'Of course.'

'Goodness, if I'd succumbed to all of the people who came
on to me while I was at Blester Combe – particularly the
tutors . . . well . . . But I had my professional situation to
think of.'

'Of course you did. Incidentally, did you notice if Al Sinclair
drank a lot when he was at Blester Combe?'

Nemone smiled coyly. 'I'm afraid Wordway courses and drinking tend rather to go together. Participants used to estimate at the beginning of the week how much they reckon they're likely to drink. We'd order that in, but almost always had to re-order by the time we got to the Thursday.'

'So Al didn't drink noticeably more than the others?'

The solid shoulders shrugged. 'As I say, they all did.'

'But did you ever see him using a hipflask?'

A beam spread across the poet's face. 'Yes, now you mention it, I do. There was an incident when he started swigging from it in one of the group workshop sessions. Some of the other participants complained.'

'So all of them would have seen his hipflask?'

'Oh yes, he was always flashing it around. Horrible battered old pewter thing.'

Jude registered the importance of that information, but didn't have time right then to process it. She changed direction. 'On the course that Burton – Al Sinclair – attended, I've heard that there was apparently a crew there making a film of the week?'

'Yes.' Nemone Coote's face clouded. 'I remember them.'

'Did they make themselves difficult?'

'Not exactly. But they showed very little interest in how a place like Blester Combe is run, you know, the logistical challenges of keeping the show on the road. They concentrated completely on the course, the tutors and the participants. Which must've made for a very unbalanced documentary about the work of the Wordway Trust. I didn't watch it when it went out. I knew there'd be nothing there that I didn't know.

'The two who made the film were very arrogant, in the way only television people can be. I'd actually gone to the effort of writing a *haiku* about the running of Blester Combe, but they showed no interest in recording it. Huh, very short-sighted. It's actually in my collection, *On Yer Haiku*, published by Pagan Libation Press.' This time she didn't even bother to ask whether Jude had read it.

'But nothing is wasted. I transmuted the unpleasant experience of meeting those television people into one of my most trenchant poems – *Square Brains for Square Eyes*, which I published under my own imprint, Bald As A Coote Press. That's one of the great benefits of being an artist, you know: the way you can channel your own traumas into your work. There's a poem I wrote on that very subject, which is in *A Tock For Every Tick*, another Bald As A Coote publication – I find self-publishing works best for me these days; it gives the poet so much more freedom to—'

Jude really felt she had to cut to the chase now. 'Sorry to interrupt you, Nemone, but I wanted to ask if you remembered another participant on the same course as Al Sinclair – someone called Steve Chasen?'

The poet shook her head. 'Name doesn't mean anything to me.'

'Keen to write science fiction? Also very keen on a drink or two?'

'Jude darling . . . That could describe almost all the participants who come on Wordway Trust courses. I remember the odd one with a spark of brilliance – like Burton St Clair – but the rest of them, I'm afraid, melt into an indistinguishable mass.'

'Steve Chasen might have been antagonistic towards Burton?'

Another shake of the head. 'We're talking quite a few years ago.'

'Of course.'

Nemone downed the remains of her Guinness.

'Can I get you another one?'

She looked at her watch. 'No, thank you, Jude. My lift'll be here in a minute.'

'Ah. Well, there is just one other thing I need to ask . . .'

'Yes?'

'On that course, did Burton St Clair ever mention that he was allergic to walnuts?'

'Oh, my God! Did he ever mention anything else? He mentioned it in his application form for the course, he mentioned it again in our first evening Meet-and-Greet session. He mentioned it before every meal, checking that there wasn't a trace of walnut in anything that was about to pass his lips. And he prided himself on the fact that his was an allergy to *walnuts*, not a *peanut* allergy like so many common people suffered from. I tell you, no one who spent that week at Blester Combe went away not knowing about Burton St Clair's walnut allergy.'

'Ah. Thank you. Who were the tutors that week, Nemone? Do you remember?'

'Well, I do, actually, because one of them was rather sweet on me. Nothing happened, of course, because of my professional position, but . . . well. The tutors were . . .' She mentioned two crime writers whose names meant nothing to Jude. But then very few crime writers' names would have meant anything to her.

'And they would have heard about the walnut allergy too?'

'Oh, certainly. Tutors always eat with the participants. There would have been no escaping it.'

'So it's just the two tutors? Nobody else comes in during the week?'

'They have a guest speaker on the Thursday evening.'

'Oh?'

'Might be another writer. Sometimes they book a publisher or an agent.'

'And that week?'

Nemone Coote looked up towards someone who had just arrived. Jude turned to see an inoffensive-looking man, swaddled in a tweed coat and fur hat with ear-flaps.

'Nearly done, darling,' said the poet. 'My husband Keith. This is Jude.'

'Pleased to meet you,' he said in a voice as inoffensive as his appearance.

Nemone Coote gathered up her considerable bulk as she rose from her seat. 'Well, pleased to meet you, Jude. Thanks for the drink.' Keith Coote looked at his watch. 'Yes, darling, we're on our way.'

Jude rose to block their exit. 'Sorry, just one thing – who was the Thursday guest speaker on that course?'

'Oh, they went for an academic that time. A specialist on old-fashioned crime fiction. I've seen her since then actually, when I was doing some work at the University of Clincham. Her name was Professor Nessa Perks.'

To digest the implications of this news, Jude went to the bar and ordered another Sauvignon Blanc from Ted. 'Carole not with you today?'

'No.'

'Up in Fulham with the grandchildren?'

'No, she's . . . er . . . I'm sure she'll be in soon.'

Another pang of guilt accompanied Jude back to her seat. Perhaps she should call Carole on the mobile, invite her along to share her recent discoveries? But Jude wanted to think for a while on her own before she did that.

As she sipped her Sauvignon Blanc, she realized that what she'd learned from Nemone Coote must bring Nessa Perks into any list of potential suspects. Here was a woman who spent her life teaching about the connections between the fictional crime on which she was an expert and the real-life crime which the police had to deal with every day. Was it possible that her obsession had led to her trying an experiment? To see if she could get away with committing a real crime based on some Golden Age template? It was at many levels a daft idea, but still intriguing.

Jude was aware of someone coming across to collect Nemone's empty Guinness glass from the table. She looked up to see it was Zosia.

Jude's surprise was as nothing compared to the bar manager's. The girl blushed to the roots of her blonde pigtails. 'I am sorry. I did not expect to see you here.'

'No, Zosia. It's not a usual time for me.' Looking closely, Jude realized how haggard the girl was. No amount of make-up could mask the dark circles under her red-rimmed eyes. The older woman reached out an arm. 'Come and sit down, Zosia.'

Wordlessly, the girl did as she was told. An instinctive arm went round her shoulders. 'What is it? Still Uncle Pawel?'

'Yes. And also, what you think of me, Jude.'

'What *I* think of you?'

'Now you know I am a liar.'

'Sorry?'

'I tell you I do not work on Tuesday. That is true, but only partly true. Tuesday I am not here during the day. The evening I work.'

'I see.' The girl looked away as Jude joined the logic together. 'Which means that a week ago you were here. You weren't cooking *kopytka* for Uncle Pawel in your flat?'

'No.'

'Which means he has no alibi for that evening?'

'No.'

'When did you last see him?'

'Lunchtime last Tuesday. I cooked for him then.'

'*Kopytka*?' Zosia nodded. 'And you haven't seen him since?'

She shook her head. 'But I was hoping, Jude, perhaps you get a clue to where he is. Perhaps you hear something from your friend . . .?'

Jude was sorry to see the light of hope die in the girl's eyes as she told her the results of Karla's researches.

'So, this Lennie has no idea where Uncle Pawel is?'

'No. Just that he is in possession of an expensive silver hipflask. A hipflask in which, as it happens, the police are likely to be very interested.'

'Why are the police involved?'

'I'm sorry, Zosia, to have to tell you this . . .' And Jude quickly outlined how Uncle Pawel's possession of the hipflask could tie him to the scene of Burton St Clair's murder.

'But he would not kill someone he did not know. He would not kill anyone! My uncle may sometimes drink too much, but he is not a murderer!'

'I'm sure he isn't. He might, however, have information that could be very relevant to the police's enquiries. Incidentally, Zosia . . .'

'Yes?' The girl was now very near to tears.

'If your Uncle Pawel did want to sell something of value, where would he be likely to turn?'

'I don't know.'

'Lennie said he'd mentioned the name of someone Polish.'

'Oh?'

'I don't think he could get the name right, but he thought it sounded like "Milo".'

All of the colour left the girl's face. 'It wasn't "Milosz", was it?'

'Could have been. "Milo" was as near as Lennie got. Why, what's the matter? If it *was* "Milosz" . . .?'

'Milosz Gadzinski is a major crook, operating along the South Coast. He is the kind of man who gives the Polish a bad name.

He makes most of his money by exploiting people of his own nationality, particularly those who have just arrived in this country. Drugs, housing scams, people-trafficking. If Uncle Pawel has got involved with Milosz Gadzinski, it is very bad news for him.'

'It may not be the same person,' said Jude, in an attempt at reassurance. 'All we've got to go on is a name that sounds like "Milo". There are all kinds of other possibilities for—'

She was interrupted by the ringing of her mobile phone.

'Yes.'

'Jude, this is Karla. I've just had contact from Lennie. A friend of his reckons he knows where Pawel can be found.'

Karla parked outside the Crown & Anchor within twenty minutes. Through the front window, Jude saw the Micra arrive and was instantly up and ready. Zosia had made her excuses to Ted Crisp. There was no way she wasn't going with them.

The route which Karla drove seemed ominously familiar. From the pub, along the seafront to the West. But she stopped before she reached Fethering Library. Stopped near the shelter Jude had walked past almost exactly a week before.

It was bitterly cold and the cloud cover was too thick for the moon to penetrate. Karla parked the car facing the sea, so that the headlights outlined the broken-glassed metal framework.

The three women did not speak; the only sound was their footsteps on the shingle.

Zosia got there first. As she rounded the corner of the shelter, she let out a cry of almost animal pain.

Karla and Jude were not far behind. They heard her sobbing as she rushed forward to cradle the emaciated figure on the ground.

The Micra's headlights caught gleams from the fresh blood.

Uncle Pawel was not moving.

TWENTY-FOUR

As the ambulance bore the old man and his niece off to hospital, Jude and Karla watched its lights dwindling along the seafront.

The paramedics had confirmed that Uncle Pawel was still alive, but their manner suggested they did not believe that state of affairs would last for long.

Fortunately, the police who'd been summoned were just an on-duty patrol in a Panda car. They had nothing to do with Detective Inspector Rollins's investigation and, so far, no connection had been made between the death of Burton St Clair and the attack on Uncle Pawel. Jude doubted whether that situation would continue, but was grateful that all the police asked for from her and Karla were contact details.

'Do you think Pawel'll make it?' asked Jude, as they walked towards the Micra.

The other woman's expression was dourly sceptical. 'It doesn't look likely. I've seen a lot of head injuries and his are pretty bad. Might be a case of hoping he doesn't make it, anyway. I can't think he'll have much quality of life after that lot.'

It was a grim assessment, but Karla had seen too much of the real world to speak anything but the truth. And maybe she was right. Uncle Pawel seemed to have been doing his best to destroy his life. Prolonging it might just be a form of cruelty. If he couldn't cope while in possession of his faculties, was he likely to do any better when suffering from brain damage?

When they got back to Woodside Cottage, Jude thanked her for the lift and offered a cup of coffee, but Karla refused. She had to get to Littlehampton for an alcohol self-help group meeting.

Jude expressed further gratitude for the help she'd been given in finding Uncle Pawel, but could tell it wasn't being taken in. For Karla, the evening represented another failure.

The old man was someone she should have helped, and she hadn't got there in time to do so.

As the Micra drew away, Jude started up her garden path, then changed her mind and went to knock on the door of High Tor.

Any frostiness Carole might have demonstrated that morning quickly melted in the warmth of her curiosity. She couldn't wait to hear what her neighbour had found out from Di, Nemone and Zosia.

'So where does that leave us?' she asked, as Jude concluded her narrative. 'Does it mean that Pawel committed the murder?'

'Not the way I see it.'

'But if he had Burton St Clair's hipflask . . .'

'We don't actually *know* that it was Burton St Clair's hipflask he had.'

'Oh, come on, Jude.'

'Yes, I agree, it's very likely, but the hipflask hasn't been found.'

Carole snorted. 'Going back to my question: do you think that Pawel killed Burton St Clair?'

'I really don't. That murder required a degree of planning that I don't think the old boy would have been capable of. Anyway, I'm sure he had no connection with Burton. Which means he couldn't possibly have known about the walnut allergy or any of that stuff.

'No, I think the most likely scenario is that Uncle Pawel, who we know had been in the shelter that Tuesday evening, wandered up to the library, after Burton was dead, and saw the hipflask in the unlocked car. He recognized it might be valuable; maybe he even hoped it still had some booze in it, so he took it. The question is, where the hipflask is now.'

'Presumably it was taken from the old boy by Milosz Gadzinski or his thugs when they beat him up?'

'But why would they beat him up?'

'To get the hipflask. He'd presumably contacted them to say he'd got a valuable silver hipflask and wanted money for it. They went to find him, having decided that they'd take it from him without giving him anything for it. The old man put up a fight. They beat him up.'

Carole sat back, content with the sequence of her logic, but when Jude didn't respond, said, 'Why? Do you have an alternative explanation?'

'I'd prefer to think of the two crimes as connected.'

'They are connected, Jude. By the hipflask. As you say, Pawel must have stolen it from Burton St Clair's unlocked car, and it was because he had it that he was attacked by Milosz Gadzinski's gang.'

'What makes you so sure it was them who attacked him?'

Carole was getting exasperated. 'Really, Jude, we're just going round in circles. Milosz Gadzinski's gang attacked Pawel because he'd told them that he had the hipflask! Come on, do you have an alternative scenario?'

'Yes. Whoever murdered Burton St Clair knew that he – or she – had contaminated the hipflask with chopped walnuts or walnut oil or walnut extract. His or her plan worked. Burton died. But the next bit of his or her plan was to remove the only piece of incriminating evidence – the hipflask – from the BMW and destroy it . . . possibly by throwing it into the sea.'

Carole caught on. 'So you're suggesting that the murderer came back to the car and found no sign of the hipflask?'

'Exactly. Which might have been good news or bad news, depending on who had got the wretched thing. But if our murderer found out for certain who did have the hipflask . . . well, that person immediately represented a danger. The person now in possession might even have witnessed the murderer doctoring the hipflask earlier in the evening. The person, once they had been identified, therefore had to be eliminated.'

'And Pawel was attacked by the same person who killed Burton St Clair?'

'That's the way I see it, Carole.'

'Hm. So who do we talk to next?'

'I think there's more information to be got out of Steve Chasen.'

From their previous encounter, Jude remembered that God's gift to science fiction worked weekend night-time shifts at

Sainsbury's on Friday, Saturday and Sunday. She also remembered that he was 'one of those people who can't go into a pub and not have a bevvy.' It therefore seemed a safe assumption that he might agree to meeting for a drink in the Crown & Anchor on a Tuesday evening.

So it proved.

She could hardly believe that only a few hours had elapsed since she had left the pub with Zosia. The shock of discovering Pawel's bloodied body made that departure feel like a very long time ago.

Steve Chasen was dressed in Doc Martens and different camouflage patterns – clearly, he had a whole wardrobe of them at home – and he turned out, perhaps unsurprisingly, to be a lager drinker. Having introduced Carole, Jude went to the bar and ordered a pint of Stella and two large Sauvignon Blancs. In the absence of Zosia, Ted Crisp served them, but that was no hardship. On a cold January Tuesday, the Crown & Anchor had very few customers.

When they were settled with their drinks, Jude said formally, 'It's very good of you to agree to meet us, Steve.'

'No problem. Anything I can do to help.' There was caution in his voice. Jude got the feeling he'd agreed to meet so readily because he wanted to assess how much they knew, and whether they had found out about information he had been concealing.

'When we talked last Friday,' Jude went on, 'you said you'd never met Burton St Clair before he came to the library on Tuesday.'

'That's right.'

'We have reason to believe that your memory on that may be faulty.' This from Carole, who was very good at playing Bad Cop when required.

'I don't know what you mean.'

'Jude talked to a woman called Nemone Coote.'

He shook his head. 'Never heard the name – and it's not the kind you'd forget, is it?'

Jude took over. 'Nemone Coote was Centre Director at the Wordway Trust house called Blester Combe where you attended a crime writing course some fifteen years ago.'

'Oh God, yes. I do vaguely remember her. Big butch lady, looked like a lezzie but was actually straight.'

'What a good memory you have when it's jogged,' Carole observed acidly.

'I can't be expected to have instant recall of people I met fifteen years ago,' Steve Chasen whined in self-justification.

'Perhaps not,' said Jude, 'but maybe another jog to your memory might help you recall a fellow participant on the course?'

His brow furrowed. 'We are talking a long time ago.'

'Burton St Clair was on that same course.'

'What!'

'Back then he would have been calling himself Al Sinclair.'

'Oh. Blimey!' He struck his head with the heel of his hand. 'I do remember someone called Al. It's all first names on Wordway courses, so I'd never have known his surname. But now you mention it, yes. I seem to remember he used to write crime novels under a pseudonym and paid for them to be vanity-published, if we're talking about the same person. And are you telling me that guy became Burton St Clair?'

As a piece of acting it would have been a shoo-in for a Golden Raspberry Award. Carole and Jude looked at him sceptically.

'The fact that you had met Burton St Clair before,' Carole observed, 'does put rather a different complexion on the events of last week, doesn't it?'

'I don't see why,' he said aggressively.

'I think you do, Steve,' said Jude. 'Nemone Coote told me that Burton was always going on about his walnut allergy. No one who'd been on that course could have avoided knowing about it. And you—'

'Oh, no.' He held up his hands to stem her flow. 'I see where this is going. If you're trying to shift the blame for murdering the bastard on to me, then you are very definitely on the wrong track.'

'Have the police interviewed you yet?' asked Carole.

'No.'

'Because when we spoke on Friday,' Jude recalled, 'you said they'd left a message asking you to make contact.'

'Which I duly did the next day. They said they might need to talk to me at some point, but I haven't heard anything since.'

'Hm.'

There was panic in his eyes. 'Why, you're not planning to contact them about me?'

'No, no,' Jude soothed.

'It wouldn't be our place to do that,' said Carole piously. 'On the other hand, it is rather interesting how much information you have withheld.'

'I haven't withheld anything! Like I say, the police haven't even spoken to me.'

'No, but you've withheld information from Jude. You've lied to Jude, in fact. Lied about not knowing Burton St Clair before last Tuesday, lied—'

'Look, I told you I didn't know it was the same bloke!'

'Lied about not knowing he had a walnut allergy.'

'If I want to lie, I'd have thought that's up to me – and certainly if the only people I'm lying to are a couple of nosy old biddies like you two. I haven't lied to the police. If they question me, I'll tell them the truth.'

'I'm glad to hear it,' said Carole drily.

'But I still don't like the way you're trying to pin this murder on me.'

'We're not trying to pin anything on you,' said Jude. 'We're just trying to get to the truth.'

Carole picked up the line of thought. 'And to do that, it makes sense that we should look for someone who was antagonistic towards the murder victim, who knew about his walnut allergy, who knew he always carried a hipflask, who—'

'Stop this, will you! Just bloody stop it! You're sounding like something out of a Golden Age detective story.'

'Oh, you know about them, do you?'

'Yes. When the library's Writers' Group was going, we had a session on Golden Age crime fiction. Bloody load of nonsense. That's not proper writing.'

No, we've already established, thought Jude, the only stuff you regard as 'proper writing' is your own. But she didn't say anything.

'Did you just do this Golden Age session amongst members

of the group?' asked Carole. 'Or did you have an outside speaker?'

'We had that batty Yank from the University of Clincham.'

'Nessa Perks?'

'That's her. She was at the talk on Tuesday, and all.'

'Yes,' said Jude. 'And what did she talk about in this Golden Age session?'

'Oh, some cobblers about old-fashioned whodunits being full of good ideas for real-life murders. She said she knew a Golden Age book that would tell anyone how to commit the perfect murder.'

'Did she tell you the book's title?' asked Carole.

'Yes, I remember it well. It was *Best Served Cold*. By G. H. D. Troughton.'

TWENTY-FIVE

On their return from the Crown & Anchor, the two women parted at their respective front gates, agreeing to make contact early on the Wednesday morning to see where they should go next with their investigation.

When she got inside Woodside Cottage, Jude felt a wave of exhaustion sweep through her. She knew it was delayed shock from the discovery of Uncle Pawel in the shelter. That thought reminded her of his plight. Was it possible that he was still clinging on to life in Worthing Hospital? She texted Zosia to send support and ask for a bulletin, but got no immediate response.

On other occasions Jude would have relaxed herself with a hot bath, candles and essential oils, but that evening she felt too wiped out. Pausing only to pour herself a massive Scotch, she went upstairs and collapsed into bed.

Next door at High Tor, Carole was wakeful. Though they'd agreed they could make no more investigative progress till the morning, Carole wasn't so sure. There must be something she could do. And, still miffed about her unequal participation in the case, she determined to do it.

She felt only a token pang of guilt about resorting to Amazon rather than waiting to use the West Sussex library service. It was an e-book she wanted, after all. She wouldn't be able to get that from Fethering Library.

Her search was surprisingly easy. Yes, *Best Served Cold* was listed. And yes, it was available as an e-book. In fact, it turned out that, with the revival of interest in Golden Age crime fiction, a lot of long-lost gems from the time were readily available.

It was a matter of moments for Carole to have the text downloaded on to her laptop.

She settled down to read for the rest of the evening – or into the night, if that seemed to be necessary. And with the opening paragraphs of the book she was instantly back in the Golden Age.

Pre-prandial drinks were taken in the library of Threshton Grange. With Dexter Hogg as his host, Sir Gervaise Montagu anticipated being introduced to the usual collection of City idlers and downright bounders who people the weekend parties of the lesser gentry. His expectation was not disappointed. There were few gentlemen present who had been to the right schools, but those who had must subsequently have let down the high principles of those academic establishments and the basic tenets of good form. Even with ladies present, most of the conversations Montagu overheard were on the vulgar subject of money.

Such certainly was the theme of Count Alexander Frisch, to whom Dexter Hogg introduced him with almost fawning enthusiasm. As they shook hands, Montagu caught the distinct whiff of brandy on the man's breath. Since the Threshton Grange butler Pinke had yet to begin serving drinks, this meant Frisch must keep a secret cache of the French elixir in his bedroom. Having already marked the man down as a bounder, Montagu now suspected he might be dealing with a cad as well.

'We have only to cast an idle eye around this room,' said Frisch, 'to see that we are among men of the world, whose brains are in tune with the mechanisms of

*international finance.' The man's accent was German,
something that did not endear him any further to the
bulldog spirit of the amateur sleuth. 'Monarchs may
tumble, shares go down to cats' meat prices, but the
gentlemen in this room will still be turning a profit.'*

*'If you would choose to call them gentlemen,' murmured
Sir Gervaise Montagu . . .*

Carole was quickly realizing the disadvantages of reading an
e-book. For the kind of search she was making, it would have
been much easier to handle an old-fashioned volume made of
paper. On that she could have annotated, marked up, flipped
back to compare references, hurried through the irrelevant bits.
E-book technology did not allow that, so she had to read the
whole text.

Which, in this case, wasn't actually too much of a hardship.

*The scene that greeted Montagu in the billiard room was
one of abject horror. At the end away from the table, men
in evening dress stood in a circle of silence. On the brows
of some the sweat of excess glistened, but their conviviality
was no more. At their centre lay Count Alexander Frisch.
One hand still gripped desperately at the billiard cue, the
other at the chalk he had been about to apply to its tip.
His thick-lipped mouth was twisted into a rictus of surprise
and agony.*

*Sir Gervaise Montagu dropped to his knees beside
the lifeless body. 'When did the fellow fall like this?' he
demanded of the assembled throng.*

*'Only moments ago,' came the reply. 'He gasped
suddenly, like a throttled dog, and hit the floor.'*

*'There's something queer about this,' observed Montagu,
'deuced queer.'*

*He bent closer to the dead man's mouth. The smell of
brandy which he had detected earlier was still there, but
to it now was added the aroma. That of almonds.*

*The detective nodded, smiled to himself, and gave an
almost unconscious ejaculation of triumph. 'Got it, by
blazes!' he said . . .*

Carole checked her watch. It was after midnight, but she could no more have stopped reading than she could have stopped breathing. She made a note of the location of the last section and pressed on, hungry for the next relevant passage.

The police surgeon's work was done. He had made his preliminary examination in the billiard room and Count Alexander Frisch's body was now in a police van on its way towards a post-mortem. The superior officer of the local constabulary was instructing his men to collect up all of the bottles in Threshton Grange, those of the wines that had accompanied dinner, and the ones which had supplied the pre- and post-prandial drinks.

'I don't know why you're finicking about with those,' said Sir Gervaise Montagu languorously.

'Sorry, sir,' the functionary responded, 'but I know the correct procedure to be followed at a murder scene. We're looking at a case of poisoning here, sir.'

'Yes, but by collecting those bottles, you're going off full cry on a false trail.'

'I think I'll be the judge of that, sir. I've been investigating murder for nigh on thirty years, and I know the correct protocols. Any student of medical jurisprudence will tell you that, in a case of poisoning, you collect everything that you know the deceased to have drunk from and then you get them all motored off to the laboratory for scientific examination.'

'All fair and above-board, my dear fellow, yes. But are you sure you've found everything that our bird drank from this evening?'

'I have spoken to all the other gentleman who witnessed his actions, sir. I have consulted the butler, the serving men, the serving maids and the kitchen staff below stairs. There is nothing the late gentleman drank from that will not shortly be on its way to the laboratory.'

'Oh, fiddlesticks!' cried Sir Gervaise Montagu . . .

The location reference was again noted. It was nearly half-past one, but Carole read on, spellbound.

His search of Count Alexander Frisch's bedroom did not take long. Montagu scorned the contents of the dressing room, where the manservant had laid out his dead master's clothes. He scorned the chest of drawers and the wardrobe, but went straight to the valises which had been stowed on top of the latter.

Donning lavender-coloured gloves before he touched the leather, the amateur detective lowered the luggage down on to the bed. It took only a few experienced twists of buckles and studs to reveal the hidden compartment.

Inside, as he had anticipated, was secreted a silver hipflask.

His gloved hands unscrewed the top and his aristocratic nose was rewarded by the distinctive tang of almonds.

'Got you, my little beauty,' Sir Gervaise Montagu breathed to himself. 'Got you, by Jupiter!'

TWENTY-SIX

In spite of her very short night, Carole was up early the following morning and on the phone at one minute past seven. She reckoned seven o'clock was an hour when anyone should be up and awake. Jude, the recipient of her phone call, had different views on that matter, but got no chance to express them. Carole said she would be round straight away, and arrived seconds later, clutching her laptop. (This was a measure of how excited she was – normally the laptop stayed in her bedroom, as immobile as a desktop.)

'The woman must be completely out of her mind,' said Carole excitedly. 'She definitely got the idea for murdering Burton St Clair from *Best Served Cold.*'

'Sorry? *Best Served Cold*?' Jude, still swathed in night-clothes, was bleary and hardly awake.

'The book, Jude! The book Steve Chasen mentioned to us last night.'

'Oh yes. But what, are you saying you've read it?'

'I stayed up half the night reading it.'

'How on earth did you get hold of a copy?'

With a slightly smug air of superiority, Carole explained the ready availability of e-books, a technology which her neighbour had not yet felt any need to embrace.

'So what do we do?'

'What we do, Jude, is to confront Nessa Perks as soon as possible.'

'But will she want to speak to us?'

'She'll want to speak to us. She's already piqued that the police haven't taken advantage of her expertise.'

'But if she actually is the murderer, surely she'll try to take evasive action and not talk to us?'

'I'd be very surprised if she does. People like Nessa Perks think they're a lot cleverer than anyone else. She'll agree to talk to us, because she'll want to find out how much we know.'

'And if we actually accuse her of murder?'

'I'm sure she'll have a strategy worked out to deal with that too.'

'Hm.' Jude was silent for a moment, and then said, 'Don't you think we should just take the information we've got to the police?'

This totally uncharacteristic suggestion was made because she was still shaken from her dealings with Detective Inspector Rollins and Detective Sergeant Knight. She had no wish to antagonize them further.

But Carole was properly contemptuous of the idea. 'Jude, can you imagine that scene? You – or you and I – go to a twenty-first-century police detective and say that the murder she's investigating is based on a whodunit written in the 1920s. I don't know what the penalties are for wasting police time . . .'

Jude took the point.

'So, what we're going to do is . . .' said Carole, in full Home Office committee-chairing mode. 'I will text Professor Vanessa Perks straight away. Then, while I take Gulliver for his walk on Fethering Beach, you will get dressed and read the extracts I've selected from *Best Served Cold*. When I get back, we'll drive to Clincham and beard the murderess in her den.'

'And what if she hasn't got back to us by then?'

'We will still drive to Clincham and beard the murderess in her den.'

In accordance with Carole's prediction, Nessa Perks was more than ready to talk to them. As Jude took in the richly loaded bookshelves of her office, the Professor confirmed, a little peevishly, that the police had still not been in touch with her. Once again, she berated the short-sightedness of their ignoring the expert on their doorstep.

'We're actually here,' said Carole, 'because we heard about the session you did on the Golden Age with the Fethering Library Writers' Group.'

'Oh, yes, that was excellent.' The Professor preened herself. 'Quite an intelligent lot they were. I gather their meetings have been discontinued.'

'Yes. Problems of staffing and funding, I think.'

'Like everywhere else.' She shook her head, implying comparable difficulties in the academic world.

'Anyway,' Carole went on, 'one of the people in that writing group, Steve Chasen . . .'

'I'm not sure that I know the name.'

'In the Writers' Group,' said Jude, 'I'm sure he would have talked about his own science fiction writing. And also, he was the one who got very rowdy after Burton St Clair's talk.'

'Oh yes, I know who you mean. I just wasn't aware of his name.'

'Anyway,' Carole said, 'he told us you did a very interesting session on the similarities between Golden Age fictional crime and contemporary real-life crime.'

'As you know, it's a matter to which I have devoted a considerable amount of research. I am an expert on the subject. In fact, at the risk of blowing my own trumpet . . .' (Carole reckoned it was a risk the Professor took all the time – and with great relish.) '. . . I might say I am *the* expert on the subject.'

'And at that session,' Carole went on, 'you concentrated on one book. *Best Served Cold* by G. H. D. Troughton.'

'Yes. The perfect illustration of my thesis.'

'An illustration whose relevance has only been increased by recent events?'

Nessa Perks nodded vigorously. 'Yes, yes. Burton St Clair's murder played it out to perfection. Perhaps I should give you a synopsis of the plot . . .?

Carole held up a hand. 'No need. I did actually read the book last night.'

'Well, I am sure you enjoyed it hugely.' The Professor uncoiled her long body from her swivel chair and moved unerringly to the right section of the bookshelf. She pulled out the relevant volume. 'First Edition, 1921. Published by Thomas Nelson and Sons. Same publisher who also did *Trent's Last Case*, of which I also have a first edition here. Dust jacket of *Best Served Cold* a little torn, otherwise excellent condition.'

Carole and Jude exchanged looks. Both were thinking the same thing – that Nessa Perks had actually volunteered the connection between the book and the recent murder. By implication, she must have known that the fatal walnut traces had been in the hipflask rather than a wine bottle. That information had not been released by the police in any of their press conferences. So surely the only way the Professor could have known it was if she had actually committed the murder?

She put the copy of *Best Served Cold* on her desk and sat back down. 'This is obviously very exciting for me.'

'What is?'

'Well, having my thesis incontrovertibly proved. There have been other instances of real-life murders apparently being inspired by crime novels, but the connection is always a bit vague. I mean, the most commonly quoted one is Agatha Christie's use of thallium as a murder method in *The Pale Horse*, and the fact that the notorious Graham Young poisoned his victims with it. There are coincidences there. In 1961, Young was fourteen, and that's when he started experimenting with thallium. *The Pale Horse* was published in the same year. But the connection was never proved. Young certainly never said that's where he got his ideas from.

'But this case is much better.' The Professor smiled triumphantly. 'There is absolutely no doubt that the method of killing Burton St Clair was taken from G. H. D. Troughton's *Best Served Cold*.'

Both women were amazed by her words. There was no doubt

about her level of academic satisfaction. And she was certainly sufficiently unhinged to discount any moral considerations in the cause of proving her thesis. But would she really take her obsession as far as murder?

Jude decided to go off on a different tack. 'Do you know a woman called Nemone Coote?'

'I have encountered her. Local self-published poet. Did a bit of work for the Creative Writing course here, but her contract wasn't renewed.'

'That's her. But do you remember meeting her fifteen years ago when she was Centre Director at the Wordway Trust's house in Wiltshire?'

'No.' Nessa Perks looked genuinely puzzled by the question. 'I do remember going to Blester Combe as guest speaker on a crime-writing course, but I have no recollection of meeting any of the permanent staff. I'm not saying I didn't meet her, but she didn't make any impression. As an academic, travelling to conferences and all that stuff, one does meet a very large number of people.'

'Of course,' said Jude.

Carole felt it was her turn to speak. 'And were you aware that the participants on that course included the Steve Chasen we've just been talking about, and Burton St Clair?'

'Absolutely not. When you do that guest speaker slot you don't really get to know anyone. I arrived at Blester Combe late afternoon, was plied with a few glasses of wine, then had a rather nasty dinner cooked by the participants. More wine, did my talk, questions afterwards. But I didn't get the names of any of the people there. Some of them were clearly going to be drinking into the night. I was asked if I wanted to join them, but opted for an early night. And my taxi to the station arrived the next morning before anyone was up.'

What she said sounded totally convincing, but then a liar who had immersed herself in Golden Age crime literature would have mastered the skill of sounding totally convincing.

'While that particular course was on,' Jude persisted, 'there was a television crew at Blester Combe making a documentary about the Wordway Trust. Do you remember that?'

'Yes, I do. They took some footage of my talk. I saw it when the programme was screened later in the year. And, though I say it myself, I did come across rather well. Not only on top of my subject – which of course I always am – but I looked very engaging too. It was strange. After the programme went out, I had expected to receive offers to front television series, but I suppose the right people didn't see it. Because some of the so-called academic women they do get as presenters are very inferior intellects. I know I could do a very much better job than them.'

'I'm sure you could,' said Carole drily. She was getting rather sick of listening to the woman's self-aggrandizement and wanted to get on to the business of accusation.

'Going back to the film crew . . .' Jude persisted.

'Yes?'

'You talked to them?'

'Oh, certainly. I asked the director about potential openings in television for someone like me, and he agreed that I was a natural.'

'And, look, I know you didn't get the names of any of the participants, but did Rodge actually mention the fact that one of them was allergic to walnuts?'

'Rodge? Sorry, who's Rodge?'

'The director who was making the film.'

'No, his name wasn't Rodge.'

'Oh?'

'No, funny, I met him again recently, as it happens. His name was Oliver Parsons.'

TWENTY-SEVEN

W hat do we do?' asked Carole, as she steered the Renault out of the University of Clincham campus. 'Go straight round to his place? Fix to meet him somewhere?'

'We don't do either yet,' Jude replied. 'My dealings with Detective Inspector Rollins have got me worried about how easily the truth gets distorted. I want to be absolutely sure that we've got our facts right before we make any accusations.'

'Very well,' said Carole, wishing her neighbour would speak a little less gnomically. 'Where do we go?'

'We go back to the library.'

So that was where she drove them. Nothing was said on the twenty-minute drive.

Carole parked the Renault in the Fethering Library car park. When they got out, both women wrapped their coats firmly around them. The wind stung their faces as it whistled acidly up from the sea. Carole started towards the library doors.

'No,' said Jude. 'We're not going there.'

Eveline Ollerenshaw's house was rather as they had expected it to be. The year 1997 had been the significant one in her life. That was when her husband Gerald had 'passed on', and since then no redecoration had taken place and no new furnishings had been brought in. It was a relatively short time ago, less than twenty years, but the place felt as though it was in a time capsule.

Evvie seemed unsurprised to see them. She invited them into her front room and insisted on going to make tea. Though it was still in theory daytime, that Wednesday in Fethering would never properly come alight. Since they'd come into the house, rain had started and was slashing icy diagonals across the window panes.

The front faced out towards the sea. Dunes cut off sight of the beach, but a sullen grey line of horizon showed, only slightly lighter than the grey sky above.

More interesting, though, to Carole and Jude, were the windows facing to the left of the front room. As Evvie had suggested, they provided a perfect viewpoint over the library car park. If they were matched by bedroom windows on the floor above, from there surveillance would be even better.

The old lady tottered in with tea and all the trimmings, including a home-made cake. The loaded tray looked very precarious in her thin, veined hands, but the two women knew better than to offer any assistance.

When they had been equipped with cups of tea, when Jude

had accepted a slice of coffee cake and Carole had refused one, Evvie settled into her regular armchair, which looked straight out towards the library. 'Well,' she said comfortably, 'I suppose you want to talk to me about what happened the night Burton St Clair died.'

'That would be very helpful if you wouldn't mind,' said Jude.

'Have the police talked to you about it?' asked Carole.

'Oh yes, they did.' The old lady sounded pleased at having been the centre of attention for a while. 'They came to see me the next day . . . well, the day the body was found.'

'Last Wednesday?'

'That's right. Obviously, because of this house's geographical location, if anyone was going to have seen anything that happened that night, I'd be the one, wouldn't I?'

'Yes,' Jude agreed. And then asked, with some urgency, 'And did you see anything?'

'Well, there are really two questions there, Jude.'

'How do you mean?'

'There's the question of whether I saw anything, and there's the question of whether I *told the police* that I'd seen anything.'

'And you're saying the answers to the two questions are different?'

'Yes, I am, Jude.'

'Are you saying in fact that you lied to the police?' asked Carole, whose loyalty to her former employer, the Home Office, was prone to come up at such moments.

'I didn't lie to them so much, as I didn't tell them the complete truth.'

'And why was that?' Carole's tone was still harsh. 'Did you have something to hide?'

'No, no,' the old lady replied. 'Someone of my age hasn't a lot to hide. I just didn't really want to be involved with the police.'

'Oh?' Carole had the skill of putting quite a lot of accusation into a monosyllable.

'Why didn't you want to be involved?' asked Jude, more gently.

'Well, it goes back to an experience my late husband Gerald had. He was always a very law-abiding man. Brought up that way, and he spent his career in insurance, so he was never going to break the law, was he? But there was a scandal at the firm he worked for, a scandal to do with car insurance.'

'What happened?'

'It involved a company of panel beaters – you know, car-repair people?'

'We have heard of panel beaters,' said Carole, in a manner testy enough to prompt a look of mild reproof from Jude. They were both desperate for the information that Eveline Ollerenshaw had to reveal, but the old lady had to be allowed to deliver it at her own pace.

'Well, these panel beaters had got into the habit – the criminal habit, it should be said – of making the damage to cars that were brought in for repair rather worse than that caused by the original accidents.'

'So that the insurance companies were charged more than they should have been?'

'Exactly, Carole. And there was some deal whereby the extra money was divided up between the owner of the vehicle and the panel beaters.'

'There have been scams like that around,' said Jude, 'as long as there has been car insurance.'

'Oh yes. But for this particular fiddle to work, when the police investigated it, they reckoned there had to be someone on the inside.'

'Someone in the insurance company?'

'Yes.' Resentful of Carole's hurrying her, Eveline Ollerenshaw deliberately slowed down her narrative. 'Well, the thing was, because Gerald worked in the car insurance section of the company, and because it was a very small department, for some time there was suspicion that he might have been involved in the fiddle. Of course he wasn't – and eventually it was proved that he wasn't. The rotten apple was a junior clerk – wide boy from the East End; he should have been the first suspect straight away – but Gerald was very much upset by the episode. He said it showed how easily lies get believed as truth, and how easy it would be for a miscarriage of justice to take place. He never forgot it.'

Evvie was silent for a moment, lost in recollection. Then she pulled herself back to the present. 'Anyway, thereafter Gerald always discouraged me from doing anything to help the police. So when that Detective Inspector Rollins and her gawky sidekick came round here to ask if I'd seen anything during the night in the library car park . . . No, of course I hadn't! I normally sleep very badly, I told them, but I had a really early night on the Tuesday and I'd slept right through. One of the best night's sleep I'd had for a long time.'

Eveline Ollerenshaw sat back in her armchair with considerable satisfaction.

Carole and Jude exchanged looks, both thinking the same thing: by what small details the processes of justice can be affected. Detective Inspector Rollins and Detective Sergeant Knight had spent more than a week in frustrating dead-end investigations, Jude had been put through a nightmare of suspicion . . . and all the time there had been a witness to the crime. A witness who, for a reason that didn't stand up to any logical examination, had withheld her testimony and not revealed to the police what she had witnessed on the night in question.

Assuming, of course, that she had witnessed something on the night in question.

Jude asked first. 'So tell me, Evvie, what did you see?'

The old lady's narrative provided just what they had hoped for. It confirmed suppositions they had made, and provided new details. After a couple of supplementary questions, Carole and Jude had all the information they required.

They thanked her, refused offers of more tea and cake, and left Eveline Ollerenshaw to her loneliness.

TWENTY-EIGHT

It was the first time either Carole or Jude had seen his house. The luxury of the interior matched the expectation given by the black Range Rover parked in the open garage. A detached

Edwardian villa, it was only separated by the coast road from the grassy dunes to the west of Fethering Beach.

But there was something anonymous about the inside of the house. The cleaning had been done with efficiency rather than love. Though some of the objects – African masks, Japanese hangings, beer steins – reflected Oliver Parsons' life of travel, they gave the impression of tokens rather than mementos. Even the framed stills from his television work looked somehow unregarded. Jude wondered how different the atmosphere in the house would have been when his wife was alive. Since their first meeting in the library, the deceased woman had not been mentioned again but, inside the house, Jude felt her absence.

Oliver Parsons seemed to know why they had come, but showed no emotion stronger than a resigned amusement. Jude had phoned to check that he was in, and they had arrived in the Renault around noon. Oliver was of the view that that was a perfect time to open a bottle of champagne, and neither woman disagreed with him.

'So,' he said, after they had raised their glasses and sipped, 'you have found out my little secret?'

'I think we have,' said Carole.

'Well, congratulations. We spoke in the Hare & Hounds in Weldisham, Jude, about Golden Age amateur sleuths and policemen. This is one up to the amateur sleuths. You got there before the flatfoots.'

'You're not attempting to deny what you did?' asked Carole.

'What would be the point of that? It's a fair cop. You've got me bang to rights.' He proffered his wrists before him, as if to have the handcuffs clicked on.

'But you must have done some research,' Carole persisted. 'There's no way you could have set the whole thing up on the spur of the moment.'

'No, you're right. It became a little project for me, and the research was part of that project. Rather fascinating, actually. I got really caught up in it.'

'As you got caught up in the library Writers' Group, and the study of Golden Age crime fiction?' Jude suggested.

'Ah. You've seen through me,' he said. 'Yes. I always have suffered from a low threshold of boredom. While I was directing, that wasn't so much of a problem. There was plenty of work; each project offered new horizons, new challenges. The adrenaline junkie within me was constantly fed, constantly stimulated. As the offers of work dwindled, things got more difficult. I needed something else in my life. Tried booze for a while, even drugs. They didn't fill the void. They were just time-wasting and destructive. As you say, Jude, I picked up on the Creative Writing, studying the Golden Age, lots of other courses and things. Each time I started with enthusiasm, but after a few months, a few weeks in some cases, I still felt unsatisfied. And then I thought of having a go at murder . . .'

'Are you telling us,' asked Carole, 'that you committed murder out of boredom?'

'Yes. That's exactly what I'm telling you. I got very caught up in it.'

'And did you get the idea for your murder method from *Best Served Cold* by G. H. D. Troughton?' asked Jude.

'You really have done your groundwork, haven't you? A woman came to the Writers' Group and talked about that book.'

'Professor Vanessa Perks.'

'Oh, well done, Carole. Another brownie point for research. Yes, the book was what set my brain in motion. I liked the idea of everyone suspecting that the poison had been in a wine bottle, while all the time it was in a hipflask.'

'Though in your case you didn't use cyanide.'

'No. I didn't want to follow G. H. D. Troughton too slavishly. Wanted to add a few of my own touches. Then I saw that Burton St Clair was coming to talk at Fethering Library, and I happened to know about his walnut allergy.'

'From when you made the film about the Wordway Trust at Blester Combe.'

'I can't tell you two anything, can I? So, anyway, I'd recently heard Burton being interviewed on some radio programme about *Stray Leaves in Autumn*, and he sounded so pretentious, such a self-regarding liar, and I thought to myself: Why don't I murder the bastard? At first it was a kind of joke, but gradually the appeal of the idea became stronger and stronger. By the end, it was an obsession. I didn't know whether it would work, but I loved the idea of trying. I think if it hadn't worked, I'd have lost interest. Forgotten about him, taken up macramé or something.' His eyes glowed. 'But it did work.'

'And didn't you feel any guilt?' asked Carole, very much in Home Office mode.

He shook his head. 'None at all. The world was free of another bastard. And, what was more to the point, I had succeeded! I had achieved what I set out to do.'

'You said you did a lot of research.'

'Yes, Jude, I did. Real cloak-and-dagger stuff. I started trailing Burton St Clair, following him, particularly when he went to do literary events. I'm very proud of how I did it, actually. He never suspected for a moment that he was being followed.

'And I found out the important things I needed to find out about him. I found out that he still had the walnut allergy. I found out that he still carried a hipflask of whisky, and had a habit of taking a swig when he got into the car after a gig. And I found out that he always kept his car keys in the pocket of his leather jacket.

'I was very excited when the relevant Tuesday arrived. I'd offered Di Thompson my help in putting out the chairs, so I knew I'd have time to set everything up if all went according to plan. But I still didn't really believe it would. I wouldn't abort my mission, but I was fully prepared to have my mission aborted by external circumstances. You know, he might keep his jacket on because it was cold; I might not be able to get out to the car park unobserved: there were any number of things that could go wrong.

'But, come the day, none of them did. I kept my gloves on in the library, which was reasonable given the outside temperature. Burton's jacket was left unattended in the staff room. I helped myself to his keys, went out to the empty car park, opened the BMW and found the hipflask in the glove compartment, just as he'd left it when he was out on previous gigs. I opened it, tipped in the ground walnuts I'd brought with me, returned it to the glove compartment. The car was locked and his keys were back in his jacket pocket. And nobody had noticed a thing. Whole exercise took . . . under two minutes.'

'And then you just had to wait?'

'Yes, but you've no idea how wonderful that waiting time

was, Jude. I felt so in control. I was challenging myself, presenting myself with the ultimate challenge, in fact. For the first time since Aileen died, I felt good.'

Both Carole and Jude realized it was the first time he had mentioned his wife's name.

'But if the anaphylactic shock had killed Burton St Clair – as indeed it did,' asked Carole, 'how were you planning to remove the evidence of the hipflask from the car?'

'Ah, this was when my plan started to go wrong. After I'd supposedly left the library, I hung around in the rain, watching from that little copse next door. And the first thing I wasn't expecting was for you, Jude, to get into the car with Burton.'

'Oh, no!' said Jude suddenly.

'What?'

'That should have put me on to you. When you asked me for that drink at the Hare & Hounds, you said you knew I hadn't got a car because I'd accepted Burton's offer of a lift. But in fact you'd left the library before he made the offer.'

Melodramatically, Oliver Parsons struck his head with the heel of his hand. *'Mea culpa!* You see? I'm sorry, I am not the master criminal I thought myself.'

'Go on,' said Carole coldly.

'Very well. I must confess, I thought at that stage, when I saw Jude get into the BMW, my plans were really scuppered. I thought Burton was going to take you to your home, to his hotel . . . I didn't know where. Whether he would then take a swig from the hipflask at some other time, I had no means of knowing. All I do know was that I felt very disappointed, cheated of my triumph at the last moment.'

'So what did you do?' asked Carole.

'I drove back home and tried to console myself – unsuccessfully – with a bottle of Scotch.'

'And then? Did you return to the library?'

'Yes, I did, Carole. You guessed that, didn't you?'

Carole was about to say that his return had been witnessed by Eveline Ollerenshaw, but a look from Jude stopped her. Both were silent, as Oliver went on, 'A dog returning to his vomit, isn't that the usual image?

'So, I went back and found – in spite of my gloomy

prognostications – my plan had actually worked. There was no sign of you, Jude, and Burton St Clair was dead. I could tell from the expression on his face and the smell of walnuts from his mouth that it was the anaphylactic shock that had killed him. Yippee! I had got away with it!

'Except, of course, there was one thing wrong. My earlier plan, once Burton was dead, had been to remove the evidence from the car.'

'The hipflask?'

'Exactly, Jude. But when I look for it in the middle of the Tuesday night, there's no sign. I move Burton around in a way which I'm sure is unseemly for a dead body, but it's not there. I still don't know where it is.'

'And that's why you got in touch with me, wasn't it, so soon after Burton's death? Nothing to do with wanting to play amateur sleuths. You just wanted to keep up to date with how much I knew.'

'Sorry, Jude.' Then, gallantly, he added, 'But I did enjoy your company too.'

'Thanks a lot.' She knew he was just being polite. Since his wife's death – and indeed during her lifetime – he had had no romantic interest in other women.

'What happened to the hipflask, though?' he asked. 'Did you take it, Jude?'

'No. Burton was still alive when I got out of the car.'

'Why did you get out of the car, incidentally? In that filthy rain?'

'Because he came on to me.'

'Ah. Yes, that would figure. So where is the hipflask?'

Quickly Jude summarized the part Uncle Pawel had played in the night's proceedings. Still neither of them mentioned the confirmation they had had from Eveline Ollerenshaw of what had happened.

'And where is the hipflask now?'

'Who knows, Oliver? Possibly in the hands of some Polish gangsters?'

'Melted down by now, I would think,' said Carole.

'So I'm almost off the hook,' Oliver mused. 'No evidence against me.'

'We know what happened.' Carole's tone was stern.

'Yes, you do. And I've confessed. But have you done the proper Golden Age thing and set up some recording contraption to preserve my confession for posterity?' He looked from one to the other and knew that they hadn't. 'Which means I might get away with it. Not that I would, of course, in a Golden Age whodunit. I would be found guilty and at my trial the judge would put his black cap on and . . .' He grinned wryly. 'This is rather like the end of a Golden Age whodunit. With very few of those, though the doughty amateur sleuths have solved the mystery to their own and their readers' satisfaction, would the case stand up in court. Could you really see the Criminal Prosecution Service taking on a case in which someone was poisoned by a gas released from a glass receptacle which was shattered by a singer on a radio broadcast hitting a high C? I don't think so.'

'Are you saying you're going to deny what you've done?' asked Carole, concerned.

'It's a thought.'

'There is a witness who saw all the comings and goings of Tuesday night.'

'Is there? I'm not surprised.' He did not ask for any further details. 'As I say, rather far from the Perfect Crime, what I set up, wasn't it?'

He grinned again. 'No, I'm not going to deny anything. Mind you, I'm not going to confess anything either. Not to the police. I think going through the process of their trying to prove I did what I did might be rather fun. Not quite as much fun as committing the murder, but getting on that way.' He yawned ostentatiously. 'Anything to stave off boredom.'

There was a long silence in the nice middle-class Fethering sitting room. 'Then Jude broke it by asking, 'Why did you really do it, Oliver?'

'Ah.' He exhaled a slow sigh. 'Why?'

'It was something to do with Aileen, wasn't it?'

'You're very perceptive, Jude.' The next silence threatened to be even longer, but then Oliver Parsons said, 'It goes back to Blester Combe. Yes, when I was making the film. I hadn't met Aileen then, but she was on that crime-writing course. There was an immediate attraction between us, we exchanged phone numbers, but not much could happen while we were there. I was busy shooting the film, she was doing all those workshops and stuff. Anyway, I was only down there for a couple of days. But we both knew it was the real thing. We swore we'd keep in touch.

'Then weeks went by, months went by, I didn't hear from her. I tried ringing her number, always got voicemail, left messages, no response.

'Eventually, three months later, she rang me. Explained that she couldn't be in touch before because she'd been having an abortion.'

'Burton?'

Oliver Parsons nodded. 'He'd come on to her at the course's last night party. Got her in one of the outbuildings. It was rape,' he concluded briefly.

Neither woman could think of anything appropriate to say.

'Anyway,' he continued, 'Aileen and I agreed to put that behind us. We got married. We were very happy. But . . . Aileen couldn't have children. Something had gone wrong during the abortion. And now she's dead.'

Again, for Carole and Jude, the right words wouldn't come.

Oliver Parsons smiled a grim smile. 'In the words of G. H. D. Troughton – and many other proverbial wordsmiths before him – "Revenge is a dish best served cold."'

TWENTY-NINE

Carole didn't argue when Jude insisted that she should see Detective Inspector Rollins on her own. Carole hadn't been involved in the witch-hunt of accusation which Jude had suffered the previous week. Jude was the one who should manage its resolution. The time was set for four o'clock that afternoon.

While she was waiting for the police to arrive, Jude had a phone call from Zosia.

Worried that the girl might be about to announce her uncle's death, she was greatly cheered to hear that the old man was making good progress. He had been toughened by his years of manual labour and stood a chance of making a full recovery, though it was unlikely he would ever be able to work again.

But what made Zosia even happier was the news that Pawel's sister was going to come over to Fethering for a few weeks to nurse her brother. The prospect of spending time with her mother had raised the girl's spirits enormously. And then it was thought likely that, as soon as Uncle Pawel was fit enough to travel, he would be taken back to Poland, where his sister could look after him – and curb his excesses.

Zosia even thought that, if he could conquer the booze, there might be the possibility of a reconciliation between the old man and his ex-wife.

Jude said how delighted she was to hear the news, and how much she longed to be introduced to Zosia's mother.

The interview, like their first one, took place in the sitting room of Woodside Cottage. They took the same seats as they had on the previous occasion. The Inspector had her iPhone on her lap, and Detective Sergeant Knight was still uneasy in her presence, uncertain when an intervention from him would be appreciated.

But that afternoon, although Rollins did not at first realize it, the dynamics between the three of them had changed completely.

Jude had agreed with Oliver that she should tell the police he was prepared to make a full confession, but it became clear at the beginning of their conversation that the police thought they had been summoned to hear a confession from her.

Of this illusion, she quickly disabused them. Marshalling the information with great efficiency, she told Rollins and Knight exactly what had happened, and what had caused the death of Burton St Clair. She also told them that Eveline Ollerenshaw had agreed to confirm what she had witnessed from her bedroom window that night.

By way of a bonus, Jude also suggested that whoever was investigating the attack on Uncle Pawel might do worse than check out the activities of Milosz Gadzinski.

At the end of her narrative, a somewhat shaken Inspector said that, of course, she would have to check everything with Oliver Parsons.

'He will tell you exactly what I have told you.'

'Very well.' Rollins rose from her sofa. Mirroring her movements, Detective Sergeant Knight did the same. 'We'd better go and talk to Mr Parsons.'

'Very good idea, Inspector. He's expecting you.'

'Good. And, er, Jude . . .'

'Yes?'

'I regret any inconvenience you have been put to.'

Jude grinned. She knew that was the nearest she was ever going to get to an apology from Detective Inspector Rollins.

She was surprised how much time she needed to untwitch from the stresses of the previous week. Paranoia was not a natural state for Jude, and she hadn't enjoyed her experience of it. Some days passed before she felt sufficiently focused to reschedule the healing sessions she had postponed.

But her mind did not readily recapture its usual serenity. Some issues resolved themselves, but the one that still felt incomplete was her relationship with Megan. Though it was her former friend's lying testimony that had put her through such anguish, Jude did not feel any resentment. Pity for someone whose mind could make them behave in such a perverse way.

She and Megan needed to talk, ideally face-to-face. But an email was too easy to ignore; the initial contact needed to be made by phone.

'Hello?' Megan sounded theatrical, but guarded.

'It's Jude.'

'Oh? What possible reason can you have for ringing me?'

'I was ringing because I assume you've heard by now how Al actually died.'

'They've told me their version of what happened, yes.'

'Are you saying you don't believe that version?'

Megan let out a 'Huh', which was the audible equivalent of a shrug. 'Al is dead. Nothing's going to change that. How he died is almost a detail.'

'Just a moment, Megan. Until recently, Detective Inspector

Rollins was convinced that I murdered Al. Convinced in particular by the evidence you gave her.'

'The evidence about you having had an affair with Al?'

'Yes, of course, that evidence. Which you knew to be untrue. And I was thinking it might help, help us both, if we could meet up and talk through how you managed to convince yourself of something so demonstrably untrue.'

'Oh, what – you're proposing to heal me, are you?'

'Just talk to you. Just try to recapture the closeness there once was between us.'

'There never was any closeness between us, Jude! And certainly none once you started to steal Al away from me. If you hadn't gone to bed with him and broken everything up, Al would still be alive, and we'd still be married! That's the truth of the matter. So don't you come talking to me about trying to "recapture the closeness" between us, because it was never there! Goodbye!'

After the phone had been slammed down on her, Jude did not attempt to ring back. Megan had not been inventing lies to incriminate her old friend. In her twisted mind she had genuinely come to believe that what she asserted was the truth. There were some people it was impossible to help.

But that final telephone conversation unsettled Jude for a long time.

Both she and Carole were shocked, but at a deeper level unsurprised, to hear of Oliver Parsons' death. Arriving at his home directly from Woodside Cottage, Rollins and Knight had received no response when they rang the front doorbell. Opening the garage door to see if they could effect an entrance that way, they had been driven back by the fumes of carbon monoxide.

The paramedics who were summoned found Oliver Parsons dead in the driving seat of his Range Rover. Beside him was a fully printed-up copy of his confession.

He had achieved the classic ending to a Golden Age murder mystery.

Once the shock had subsided, Jude felt sadness but also a sense of inevitability. Oliver Parsons' life, she now recognized, had ended with the death of Aileen. Since then he had just been going through the motions.

Nor could she feel much regret over what happened to Burton St Clair. Justice, she knew, did not always conform to the strict dictates of morality.

'I should have seen it coming,' said Carole, as they sat that evening over Sauvignon Blanc in the kitchen of High Tor. Gulliver snuffled serenely in front of the Aga.

'Seen what coming?'

'What Oliver Parsons did.'

Unusually for her, Carole had brought her laptop downstairs. 'Look. I should have realized.' She turned the machine round so that Jude could see the screen. 'From the second paragraph.'

And Jude read another extract from *Best Served Cold* by G. H. D. Troughton.

> *'There's no point in being too kid-glove about this, Danvers,' said Sir Gervaise Montagu. 'You've been shown up as a wrong 'un fair and square.'*
>
> *'Hanged if I know how you tumbled to the gag.'*
>
> *'I wouldn't use the word "hanged" too lightly if I were in your shoes. You're as guilty as blazes and you'd be convicted by any court in the country.'*
>
> *'Yes, it does rather look as if I'll soon be kitted out with a hempen necktie.'*
>
> *'No way round it, Danvers old man. Unless of course . . .'*
>
> *'Yes?'*
>
> *'I'm going to take a turn around the rose garden. But I happen to know that Dexter Hogg keeps his service revolver in the top drawer of his desk right here in the library.'*
>
> *'Does he, by Jove?'*
>
> *'Yes, and his ammo too.'*
>
> *'Righty-ho.'*
>
> *'I don't need to tell you the decent thing to do in these circumstances, do I, Danvers?'*
>
> *'No, Montagu, you don't. I may be a cad and a bounder, but at least I'm British, and I know when to do the decent thing.'*